# Original Sin

Barbara Winkes

 ISBN: 978-1-0696671-6-8

*For D.*

# Chapter One

"**M**om?"

She hated how small her voice sounded. She had faced far graver and more dangerous challenges in her life. Joanna hadn't expected this phone call to be so hard. She had nothing to prove, nothing to be sorry for. Or did she?

"Who is this?"

Her apprehension gave way to confusion in a heartbeat, and a pang of an entirely different emotion. Painful. Was it possible?

"Mom, it's me, Joanna. I need to talk to you."

"How did you get this number? This is not a safe line. You shouldn't have called." The sharp tone and the palpable fear bordering on paranoia were so unlike her memory of Mary Mitchell, but somehow, her voice still felt familiar. The realization filled Joanna with longing, maybe for something that had never been real in the first place.

"You don't have to worry. Dad gave me this number. He wasn't all that happy to do it, but...here we are. I won't be in the country for much longer. If it's at all possible, I'd like to talk to you."

"I don't know," Mary said after a long pause. "What good would that do? I'm not sure what you're hoping to learn."

Her words weren't encouraging, but there was a lot between the lines making Joanna think she still had a chance. She needed to do it, if not for Mary, then for herself. She had a hard time living with loose ends.

At the other end of the room, Rue was flipping through a magazine, pretending she wasn't listening, but on alert should Joanna need her.

"I want to meet you in person, just one time. I think you owe me that much."

"Oh, honey, I owe you a lot more than that."

Given how their conversation had started, Joanna almost thought she'd imagined those words. Knowing she hadn't, left her excited, and with many more questions. This wasn't something they could solve on the phone.

"When can I see you?" Joanna asked. "Like I said, we don't have much time. Would tonight be okay?"

"I have a show, but if you're okay with that, you could come see me after."

A show. That was both fascinating and frustrating. It was quite clear where any musical talent Joanna could hope to have, came from. She had recently started to play the piano again. It was that musical talent that had made Mary leave her family behind. She hadn't become famous when she ran away with the band, but apparently, that was still her job.

"I guess we could do that. Thank you."

"We? Lawrence isn't coming. No. Rue, my fiancée is here with me."

"Oh, okay. Sure." Maybe she thought that was giving her a way out of a difficult conversation. Maybe it was Joanna who needed the way out. Had she made a mistake? None of this felt real. Perhaps she should have counted her blessings and gone home with Rue. She couldn't go back now.

"I'll see you then. It's at the Colosseum. We start at eight...I don't know if you want to be there this early. It's sold out, but I'll leave your name at the door, and they'll let you in."

"Thank you. I appreciate it. We'll be there."

"I look forward to seeing you, Joanna. It's been such a long time."

It was on the tip of her tongue to say it wasn't her fault. She held back the comment. They had only been talking for a few minutes, enough for Joanna to form an impression. Mary appeared rather detached from reality. She thought someone might be listening in on the call. She didn't seem to think the long silence between them was in any way her fault.

What if it wasn't?

If Lawrence made up reasons as to why Mary had left, why did he give Joanna her number? He wasn't looking to do her any favors. He made that clear the last few times they met.

"Is everything okay?" Rue's soft-spoken question made her realize that she had been staring into nothing since she and Mary had ended the call. Okay? That was relative.

"I guess we're going to a concert tonight."

"She's a performer? So, this is where your talent comes from."

She knew Rue meant well, but it was a chilling thought that various other features of hers might come from her parents.

"Talent, we'll see. Let me check the address, and then we can go for dinner?"

The Colosseum wasn't as big as the name might suggest, more like a cozy theater with tables and a bar but selling it out was still respectable. She was curious to see what her mother had gained when she gave up her family. Almost thirty years ago.

Joanna was still angry. But her emotions didn't matter as much as getting answers. She had waited long enough.

3

The woman guarding the door at the Colosseum gave Joanna the once over, her smile slipping slightly when she saw Rue.

"I'm here to see Mary Mitchell," Joanna said.

"I'm sorry, you're too late. Even if we hadn't closed the doors already, we're sold out."

"She said she was going to give you a heads-up. I'm Joanna. Her daughter."

The woman's eyes widened before she said, "Of course. Mary's daughter and the plus one. I'm sorry. Please follow me."

"No problem."

She led them around the building to another set of double doors and opened them. "Come on in. We'll get you a couple of backstage passes, and drinks if you like."

Joanna would have liked something strong, but she declined. "Rue?"

"I'm fine, thank you."

Joanna knew she'd need a clear head for the conversation ahead. She was beginning to doubt it was such a good idea to agree to this location. It seemed utterly inappropriate for tackling the subjects she and Mary needed to address. She couldn't help being impressed. Mary's band might not be famous, but they seemed to have a following, enough to allow her to stay in this profession.

Or perhaps it was Lawrence who allowed her to stay in it, though Joanna couldn't figure out why. He hadn't shown Joanna a lot of love at any point in her life, so what did it matter to him if Mary was in the picture or not? What did it matter to him if she was struggling?

Any attempt of hers to solve the riddle was too clouded by emotion.

They might have been late, but they were just in time for the curtain to rise. The security guard had directed them to a table in an area close to the stage. Joanna couldn't help feeling excited, even though she couldn't completely forget about the reason why they were here.

And then she laid eyes on her mother for the first time in nearly three decades. She realized she'd been holding her breath too long when the scenery blurred for a few seconds. She knew Mary's age, of course, but seeing her standing at the microphone in the form-fitting red dress, she was startled to realize how young she'd been when she married Lawrence.

"Good evening," Mary said. "I'm so glad you're all here. I hope you're going to have a lot of fun, and I also want to tell you that this is a special night for me. For the first time, my daughter Joanna is in the audience."

In the resulting applause, Joanna caught Rue wiping her eyes.

Joanna wasn't sure what to make of this announcement, or anything at this moment. Was Mary a brilliant actor? A two-faced woman? Or did she actually have a good reason to leave, other than that a ten-year-old girl didn't fit into the dreams she wanted to realize?

She might not get all the answers today, and perhaps she'd have to limit her expectations. Joanna didn't have to fear repercussions for evading questioning in the case of a serial killer's death, not this time, but she and Rue still had to make a living. Their home was the island, not here.

So. Mary Mitchell, the performer. She was good, Joanna had to give her that. One of those voices that would do reasonably well in a reality TV contest but have to drop out just before the finale. She didn't know what to think, if she should be mad or even still had the right to be. She felt herself seduced by the music, Mary's interpretation of familiar tunes, soft, haunting. Maybe a person was pre-programmed to make excuses for their parents no matter what, though she'd never fallen into that trap with Lawrence.

Mary couldn't see them right after the set, so Joanna eventually agreed to a Gin and Tonic. She and Rue stayed at their table, each of them hanging on to their own thoughts.

"There you are!"

Mary, now dressed in jeans and a button-down shirt, her hair in a pony-tail, joined them. For a few seconds, she stood, seeming uncertain about what to do next, then she pulled herself a chair. "I'm so glad you came. Really. And you must be Rue."

Rue shook her hand with a smile, though her hesitation came across clearly. Joanna decided she had to cut to the chase.

"Thank you for meeting us. I'm not sure how much you caught of the recent news, but it's been pretty turbulent times for us. We'll have to go home soon, but I realized I didn't want to leave without—"

"Without what?" Mary asked softly.

"Seeing you. Asking you why."

Why not go straight for the pressure point?

"I was hoping we could just spend a little time together." Joanna's disbelief must have shown, because she hastened to add, "I'm sorry if that wasn't what you were looking for, but that's all I can offer you. The rest...It's better if you don't know."

"What, that you were selfish and left me with Dad to follow your dreams? I know that already. I was hoping you could give me one other reason."

If those words were hurtful, it was because Joanna meant them to be. It might not be fair, but nothing about this situation was.

"I understand this from a little girl's point of view. I can't even imagine..." Mary's eyes were welling up, or maybe it was just the lamp on the table that made them appear bright. She straightened. "I admit I don't know as much about you as I should, but I know you had to make some difficult choices. I had to make difficult choices as well...I was hoping you could understand that after all the experiences you've had."

"I can't understand it when I know nothing! And going to prison certainly wasn't my dream."

"I'm really sorry. I wish things were different, but we can't change the past, can we? Just to see you here, to know you're safe and loved, it makes me happy. I never imagined I'd be able to meet you someday."

Joanna shook her head, irritated and confused at this conversation, Mary's calm tone, the words that didn't make sense. She might have neglected to ask Lawrence the right questions.

"What are you talking about? You met me. I'm your daughter. Look—I'm sorry I bothered you. This was a mistake."

She got to her feet, and Mary did as well, looking alarmed.

"Joanna, please don't leave like that. I'd like to see you again."

"I'm not sure that's possible. Again, I'm sorry."

"You could have tried."

Already on her way out, Joanna spun around. "What?"

"You were a cop. You had tools at your disposal, and I wasn't that hard to find. But you never wanted to."

She felt the heat rise, to the point of nausea. She shouldn't have drunk that Gin and Tonic so fast. What if Mary had a point? Joanna had grown up convinced that Mary had one day decided she didn't want her, didn't want life as her mother, and Lawrence Mitchell's wife. Why would she use resources the public entrusted her with?

Then again, Joanna had done worse than that.

"I did. I was just too afraid of what I would find. Good night, Mom."

Rue followed her out of the venue, struggling to keep up with her. "Joanna, wait a second."

Joanna halted abruptly and turned to her.

"Don't tell me I should go back and apologize. You saw everything. She's enjoying her life. She had no real reason—other than Lawrence was a shitty husband, but she could have taken me with her."

"Maybe she wanted to."

"I can't deal with maybe anymore. Let's forget about this and go home."

The piercing scream cutting through all other sounds around them was a clear indication that going home wasn't an option yet.

# Chapter Two

There weren't many options. Joanna gripped Rue's hand tightly, and they headed back into the direction where they'd come from, opposite of what most people were trying to do.

It wasn't even a moment's consideration. She had to make sure. And Rue, unwaveringly, would be by her side, as always. The scream had come from a place near the stage door.

The security guard from earlier was nowhere to be seen, but Joanna found Mary standing to the side with a man about her age. They were tending to a young woman who sat on a chair, looking like she was about to faint any moment. She was clutching her notepad in a white-knuckled grip. All of them appeared shell-shocked.

"What happened?" Joanna asked.

Mary swallowed hard. "It's Terry, one of my crew members. This is Carly, an intern for the Colosseum, and Jeff, my manager. Carly...She found Terry dead."

The young woman was crying quietly. Joanna nearly followed the impulse to go past the door, but Rue held her back with a pointed look.

"Dead, how? Has someone called the police?"

Mary had a manager. Joanna wasn't sure why that detail mattered to her at all, under the circumstances.

"I did," Jeff said. "It appears that he was shot. Some of the guests heard the shot and panicked...I don't blame them, these days, but it looks like whoever did this, came for Terry."

"You have reason to assume that?"

"Joanna. The police will be here soon," Rue reminded her. This wasn't her job, and even beyond that, neither of them had a reason to get involved. Mary wasn't hurt. That was all she needed to know, right?

The detectives on the case seemed to agree when they arrived only minutes later.

"I can't believe this." Theo shook his head, his partner Allison's expression somewhere between resigned and frustrated. "Why are you here again?"

"We came to see the show," Joanna said. "I thought that after all the trouble, we deserved to relax a little before we went back home for good."

"And look where that got you. Did you see anything?"

"No, but apparently there are some witnesses who heard a gunshot. The body is in there. You might want to talk to the manager." She nodded towards Jeff. "Intern found him."

"Wow. Okay."

Allison Kato found more words.

"Thank you, Joanna. I'd like to ask you two to go to your hotel now, please. If we have any more questions, we know where to find you. Good night."

As strange as it felt to hear those words, she had a point. Joanna walked over to Mary and touched her arm, feeling her flinch.

"I just wanted to make sure you were okay. Bye."

She didn't give Mary a chance to react in any way, and she and Rue could finally go back to the hotel.

The scream reverberated in her mind, following her into her nightmares where it echoed her own.

It was silly, Rue tried to reason as she was catching her breath, Joanna's hand gentle on her back.

She hadn't seen the body, or blood. A man was dead, but the circumstances where nowhere near the recent murders that had hit much too close for all of them. Revenge, maybe, or a hit. It was tragic, but it was also contained. No other monster roaming the streets, looking for a victim? She realized she was shaking. Great job freaking herself out.

"Mary has a really great voice," she said, trying her best not to burst into tears. Joanna pulled her into a close embrace.

"This was unexpected."

Rue's reaction to Joanna's understated assessment was inappropriate laughter. "You could say that. A dead body and all." She pulled back and got up from the bed to take a bottle of water out of the fridge. "Unexpected."

"Are you okay?"

"Are you?" Rue returned.

Joanna looked like she needed more time to ponder that question.

"Honestly? I don't know. Everything about this was just bizarre. She wants to see me, but she can't tell me anything? She thinks the phone is bugged, someone tricking her into—what?"

"It's been a long time."

"So, either she's trying to make herself look better by sounding mysterious, or there are other issues at work."

There was a tinge of sadness to Joanna's voice, for the time lost, or perhaps hopes she'd held on to during that time.

"I'm really sorry it didn't work out the way you hoped."

"I don't know that either," Joanna said, pensive. "When she sang...That's the way I remember her. But then I also remember this is why she left. She's right though. I believed that she had no interest in seeing me, so I didn't try to find her. At some point, I just thought she and Lawrence were the same."

Rue wanted to weigh her words carefully. After all she had no idea what it was like to be in this situation. She, too, had trouble to make sense of it all. Mary seemed genuine. Perhaps she did regret what she'd done, and if given the chance, she'd attempt true reconciliation.

That would mean they'd have to stay a little while longer.

It didn't mean, and she had to remind herself, that they'd have to get in any way involved in what happened at the Colosseum. There were many reasons as to why someone had shot one of Mary's crew members, and none of them had anything to do with her or Joanna.

"It would be hard to tell from one meeting, especially when it ended like it did," she offered. "Would you like to see her again? At this point, it doesn't matter if we postpone going home for a couple of weeks or so." It was a random number Rue had thrown out, hoping Joanna would get what she was really saying.

"I'm not sure that a couple of weeks would be enough, but I don't want to stay indefinitely. Our life is elsewhere now, and let's not forget we have a wedding to plan. The way things are now, we can have your parents there too."

True, things were fairly uncomplicated for Rue's parents now that Joanna had been pardoned by Governor O'Neal, and they didn't need to stay under the radar any longer. Rue didn't need to ask about Lawrence Mitchell. She had gotten to know her former boss well enough to know he wasn't going to change his homophobic ways, and he wasn't much touched by the fact that his daughter found love.

Mary? She might even want to perform at the wedding? Now she was getting far ahead of herself.

"Give it a couple of weeks," she said. "Meet her again, address what you need to. I'll be with you if you need me, but I don't mind giving you some space either."

"We'll figure something out." Joanna gave her a grateful smile. "Thank you."

"For what?"

"For being you and reminding me of what's real."

"I could say the same about you. And since we're awake anyway, I could think of something else to remind you."

Rue didn't want to go back to sleep and risk another nightmare. Fortunately, she and Joanna were on the same page where this subject was concerned.

They were about to go down to the breakfast room when Joanna's phone rang. She wasn't sure how to feel about hearing Mary's voice. A lot had happened between the last phone call and the present moment, most of which made her want to go home already. It might be that there wasn't a mystery to solve.

"Joanna, I need you to come here, please."

That was unexpected.

"What's going on?"

"It's been extreme since...Terry. The police keep coming back and asking me more questions—I think they suspect me."

"Why would they suspect you?"

Theo and Allison were thorough, Joanna knew that. But Mary had been with her manager, and besides, this was...yes, extreme. Like imagining someone listening in on a phone conversation? Now she wished she had asked Lawrence a whole lot of more questions. Maybe it wasn't too late.

"I don't know, but I thought, maybe you could talk to them? Terry was part of my family. I wouldn't do anything to hurt him, and neither would anyone of us...but we didn't know a whole lot about him."

Silently, Joanna weighed her options. She had planned to meet Mary again, even after the unfortunate incident. Try to clear up some of the past. Her motivation didn't go beyond that. It was a pretty big task already.

"I could come by," she offered.

"Thank you so much. I really need you here."

Spooked, Joanna ended the conversation before she could read a lot more into those words than Mary had intended. She turned to Rue, hesitating.

"I'm pretty sure this won't take long. She seems a bit freaked out."

"Imagine that," Rue said, the sarcasm not meant for Joanna, but summing up the collective experience that had brought them here.

It was an uncomfortable thought that because of Joanna, Rue had been around more dead bodies than anyone should be. Maybe it wasn't her fault. The result was the same.

"You could have breakfast, and we'll meet here later?"

"Sure. I know you'll want to talk to Theo..."

"We'll see. That's his job, not mine."

Rue gave her a half shrug. In the past, Joanna hadn't always stuck to what was her job. First it was about an old nemesis, then Rue in danger, and a couple of young women in distress who deserved so much better...

Mary didn't ask her to solve the murder. Joanna's curiosity was aimed at something else. Maybe they could both get what they wanted?

"I'll be back soon," she promised.

# Chapter Three

M ary had given her the address of a hotel. The city was a tour stop, not her home. While it didn't offer five-star accommodations, Joanna admitted to herself she was surprised once more. Mary seemed to have built a considerable career mostly covering other artists. Portraying their songs with a haunting layer of longing...

Almost like the longing that had haunted Joanna through most of her childhood, for the memory of a parent that was the opposite of Lawrence Mitchell's cold detached ways. But she was an adult now. She'd never get that time back, no matter what she'd learn about Mary's motivations.

Mary met her in the hotel restaurant where the breakfast buffet was still displayed.

"If you're hungry, please help yourself. I already paid for it."

"Thank you." Joanna was most grateful for the coffee, but the food, muffins and other pastries, eggs and meat looked amazing to her growling stomach.

Mary opened her purse and took out a leather etui, then put it back inside.

"Nowadays I can't even smoke on the terrace. Well, better for my voice anyway."

"I used to smoke," Joanna said. "I quit a while ago." She wondered if it sounded judgmental, which wasn't her intention. It was intriguing to see another thing they had in common. Musical talent. Addictive behavior.

"Good for you. How did you do it?" Mary asked, sounding as if she was genuinely interested in the answer.

*I stopped feeling sorry for myself*, Joanna almost said. While it had been true for her, she was aware it would be overly harsh and judgmental, especially given the fact that she and Mary had just reconnected. Smoking wasn't by far the biggest issue here.

"I met Rue." What if that hadn't happened? Would she have continued to go through the motions at her job, dulling the pain of dreams never realized with booze, nicotine, and casual sex? Those questions were too uncomfortable in an already awkward setting. She'd understood that she, too, deserved to be treated well. "If you don't mind, I'll get some food, and we can talk?"

"Of course. Go ahead."

When Joanna had sat down at the table again, Mary gave a heavy sigh.

"You must think I'm insane," she said.

"To be honest? I really don't know what to think. Insane is a harsh word. I think you were very young and unable to handle the responsibilities you had. Part of me still doesn't understand because...I remember you. You were kind."

"I wish kindness were enough. And I wish I could tell you all of it, but you have no idea how complicated things were, and how messy they are right now. They didn't tell me that much, but Terry wasn't who he said he was."

"What does that mean?"

"I was hoping you could talk to the detectives. I...I know a little about you, Joanna. You're still close with them. I'm scared that someone is trying to set me up for Terry's death."

"Why would anyone do that? Why would they bug your phone?" Joanna shook her head, impatient with herself, and with Mary who seemed to bring everything back to some big conspiracy.

"I can't say…"

"Yes, I got that part. I'll give Theo a call if that makes you feel any better, but I can't imagine they suspect you, especially if the guy lied to you."

"Some people will stop at nothing. You know that."

Biting her lip, Joanna told herself that she had various options. One of them was an angry retort that would bring their conversation and any chance at reconciliation to a jarring halt. Another, to count to ten and try to get to the bottom of Mary's vague hints.

"I'll talk to him. But you have to give me something."

"After the show, I met you and Rue, and then, after you left, I went to talk to Jeff."

"We heard the scream not much longer. You have an alibi then. I wouldn't worry. They have to talk to everyone."

"It's more complicated than that, but I'm so glad you're here. Now that I know you're going to take care of this…I was hoping you'd stay a little bit longer. Tell me about your life, and Rue. Are you married?"

"Not yet. We are planning to. Things have been a little wild on our side as well." Joanna was halfway through her sentence when she realized she'd gone with the change of subject, just like that. Strange to realize that part of her was still the little girl hoping for her mother's approval. Hoping for her to stay this time.

She suppressed a sigh. It was only natural that Mary was upset by the death of someone close to her, especially since it involved the police. Joanna still couldn't tell how much of it was a normal reaction, or if part of it had to do with something Lawrence had neglected to tell her.

She wouldn't put anything past him.

"That is wonderful. Now, after the pardon, would you come back to live and work here? Have the wedding here, maybe?"

"Oh, no. We're going home as soon as possible. In fact, we might be back already if it wasn't for...I really wanted to see you. And the reason I didn't look for you is that Dad told me you didn't want any contact with either of us."

Come to think of it, why would she have trusted him with anything? Before Decker, Joanna had been a different kind of cop, by the book, someone who wouldn't use department resources for personal reasons, not for a minute. Then again, it might not have been that difficult. A simple internet search might have turned up live footage, the fan base...contact information. She'd been terrified of what she might find, unable to handle another parent who might reject her, everything that she was.

"I see how he could be convincing," Mary admitted. "I almost believed that."

"But now...Neither of us needs to give him that power. Whatever else there is, you can tell me."

"I'm afraid I can't, not now. But I'm so glad you came."

"It's no problem," Joanna said, ignoring the pang of disappointment. "I'll get back to you as soon as I know more."

She knew what she needed to do. Joanna didn't plan to solve a murder. If she was going to ask a few questions, it would only be for her own—and maybe, Mary's—peace of mind.

❦

Joanna called Theo to see if he was free to meet her for a quick coffee break. She could walk into the police station without any worries, or obligations, but she preferred not to. People would still stare. She could do without that.

He came to the diner across from the station ten minutes later.

"Not that I'm not glad to see you, but shouldn't you be relaxing and enjoying your time in the city?"

"I'll still have time to do that. Just a quick question about the dead guy at the Colosseum."

"Wow." He frowned at his coffee and added more milk. "I should have known. Look, I'm really happy for you that things worked out with the governor. I didn't expect to find you right there at the next murder scene."

"That was an unfortunate coincidence. Mary is my mother. She asked us to meet at the venue and...here we are."

"Yes, here we are. Like you said, it's all unfortunate, but this guy's death has nothing to do with her, or you. So, enjoy reconnecting, and leave everything else to me and Allison."

"There's no trouble with Mary's alibi?"

"Who told you that?"

Theo had a reasonably good poker face, but she'd worked with him for too long not to see past it.

"Come on, you're not actually looking at her? She's an artist. A bit flaky maybe, something I can attest to, but she's not a murderer. There must be something else going on."

"There's a whole lot going on with this victim, but none of it is your business, or hers."

"You know what happens when you try to stall me."

"You know what happens when you abandon all rules that are in place for a reason. Do you miss prison that much?"

"That was a low blow," she said, startled by his sharp retort. "I'm just asking a few questions. She's worried you might suspect her, and frankly, I'm not sure she's the most stable person. This is tough on her. Can I at least tell her she's in the clear?"

Theo sighed. "Nothing is ever easy with you, is it? I don't think she pulled the trigger or even told anyone to. You can tell her that."

"I sense a 'but'."

"Go home, Joanna. I know for a fact there's someone waiting for you."

That was enough to chastise her. There was nothing wrong with Mary asking her for a favor, but Rue had been there for her through rather desperate times. Joanna owed her more than anyone, and right now, she was falling short on the task.

"I hope you can close this case soon."

"You and me both."

"You're right. I don't want to go to prison. I don't want that for her either."

She didn't wait for an answer.

Allison Kato had a headache. She attributed it to all the missing pieces in the case, nagging at her mind, when it should be cut and dried. Mary Mitchell's crew member, Terry Dillon, had an astonishing amount of gambling debt. It wasn't much of a stretch to assume someone had come to collect, and that they were tied to organized crime.

So far...not so good. The mere fact that he was connected to Mary Mitchell, Joanna's mother, worried her. What were the odds?

There was more to her pains than this strange coincidence. According to the witness' statements, Dillon had lived a fairly unassuming life. Yet, he had a penthouse on the top floor of a skyscraper, and a garage with a brand-new Porsche in it. If he'd had a winning streak lately, Terry Dillon had not used it to pay off his debts.

And there was this whole other life he'd apparently had before coming to work for Mary, as a shady PI with few clients.

Nothing about Terry added up.

And Joanna Mitchell was on the periphery of this mess. Allison sincerely hoped that she and Rue would be off to the island soon.

"Hi, Allison. You have a moment?"

Startled out of her musings, Allison suppressed a sigh. The fact that her partner was AWOL, and his girlfriend was standing in front of her desk, her question more like a statement, couldn't be a coincidence either.

"The question is rather, do I have a choice?"

Vanessa didn't deny that she wasn't going to take no for an answer.

"I brought you your favorite latte," she said. "You know Theo tries to avoid shop talk, but I still have friends around here. So, Terry Dillon."

"What about him?" Her headache was about to get worse.

Complicated history connected Vanessa and Joanna Mitchell, and if both of them got involved, Allison wasn't sure what that meant for her case. She couldn't be mad at Joanna, not much. She had saved her life. She wasn't amused about Vanessa interfering in any way.

"I don't know that much about him," Vanessa admitted. "What I do know is that he got in bed with the wrong people. Made a lot of money quick, spent even more and made some enemies."

"We figured out that part. Why are you here?"

"I need you to ease up a bit on Mary Mitchell."

"Did Joanna tell you to do this?"

Vanessa laughed. "Joanna would be spitting mad at me if she knew. No."

Allison had been right—this was getting worse. "Then why are you getting involved in this?"

"I have sources, reliable ones, that tell me she has nothing to do with this."

"But her stalker does?"

Vanessa tried to hide her surprise, but Allison had learned to identify minute reactions that gave people away, like her eyes widening, if only for a split-second, and her straighter posture.

"The stalker is an urban legend, right? You must understand it's a critical time for Joanna. She was damn lucky, but she can't use any distractions right now. Let's send her and Rue back home as soon as possible, and we can all enjoy the wedding."

"I'm not sure I'll be invited," Allison said as if that mattered. "I know you're still trying to make up for busting her." She held up her hand when Vanessa opened her mouth to protest. "Don't worry, I get it. But I have a murder to solve, and I'll go where the evidence leads me. Even if I need to look at urban legends. Joanna has nothing to worry about."

"I wouldn't be so sure of that, but I appreciate your honesty. Thank you for your time."

"You're welcome."

The wall beckoned him, like it always did, and he quickly went to add the latest pictures. So, it wasn't actually a wall, but an entire room. Who cared? He was amazed and proud at the progression, his chosen one, the ones that mattered, and the ones that...would be better out of the way.

Killing the first one had been easy, and a few after that, too, because no one really made the connection. Accidents, slightly suspicious deaths ruled "of natural causes." Well, maybe it had been only natural for some of them to die.

They were in the way.

Her way.

He was working his way up to the more important players. He knew he had to proceed with utmost precision, otherwise his whole plan would go up in flames.

He was no amateur—they'd all have to learn that, the police, the shadowy people surrounding her, and those closest to her.

Mary, too, would learn. After many years, their paths would finally cross.

# Chapter Four

When Joanna returned to the hotel, Rue was wearing a resigned expression.

"I'm sorry this took so long. I had a quick talk with Theo...We could meet with him and Vanessa tomorrow night."

"That's all right."

"Perhaps I could see Mary one more time. For the life of me, I don't know what to make of all this. I wish—"

"Joanna, please sit down," Rue said. "There's something I'd like to show you."

She went over to the sitting area where the open laptop sat on the table. Looking over Rue's shoulder, Joanna could see the website of a newspaper on the screen, an article dealing with the mystery surrounding Terry Dillon.

"There's not a whole lot of this that makes sense, but in any case, something strange was going on with this guy," Rue continued. "Some say he might have been blackmailing your mother."

"Blackmail her for what?" Joanna frowned. "She left her family to go sing in a band. Whatever anyone thinks of that, it's all out there. I don't think she has that many secrets—" Even as she said the words, she was reminded of Mary's intermittent strange, paranoid behavior. Did that mean there was a reason for it? She wasn't exactly in hiding. Lawrence had known where she was all this time, he just didn't care to share. That was something to worry about another time. She wasn't going to go home without confronting him on this issue.

"Like I said, not all of it makes sense, but he certainly wasn't what you think of as a typical crew member of a cover band. There was a lot of money involved."

"Yeah, that's what Theo said. But Mom—" She corrected herself right away. "Mary didn't know about any of it, at least I'm pretty sure about it. They seem to be doing okay, but no one is making millions."

"They say that he was a private investigator looking into her and that someone close to her might have...interfered."

Joanna sat on the edge of the bed, dumbfounded. If she was honest, she didn't have any room to judge, what could be the truth, and who had bent it to their advantage. But she could only think of one person who had the power to "interfere." No, that would be ridiculous. He was a bitter old man, clinging to his bigoted attitudes. He was not a murderer.

"Well, if that happened...I don't know how we could help her. I'd still like to think that we can go home by the end of next week."

"Are you sure about that?"

"Why would you ask that?" Her exclamation made Rue flinch, and Joanna felt instantly guilty. "I'm sorry, I didn't mean to snap. There is so much about Mary I don't know, and at this point, I'm not sure how far I want to go. But I still think that Theo and Allison will find the murderer. Mary left. Lawrence kept an eye on her and never told me. Apparently, this strange arrangement worked for them somehow, and it's much too late to change anything about that." Rue still looked doubtful. Joanna got up and took both of her hands in hers.

"I'm serious. We've had enough of the bad stuff. I want to go home with you. I want to marry you on the beach and have a party with our friends and family that want to be there. There's nothing left here for me."

Rue gripped her hands tightly.

"I want that too. But...if there's anything left that you need to do, I'll support you. You know that."

"Yes, I know that."

It was only a matter of how much more of the darkness she was willing to expose them to. Maybe it wasn't worth it.

Joanna tried to put those thoughts out of her mind for the rest of the day they spent in the city, like ordinary shoppers. It was a relief to be among strangers, people who were completely unaware of the chaotic months they'd lived through.

Better to leave it alone. For a while, at least.

She couldn't help wondering about the private investigator, Mary's real fears or paranoia, she wasn't sure which, and whatever Lawrence might have to do with it.

Come to think of it, no one was innocent in this. She could have pushed harder for answers, years ago. But then every attempt would bring back the girl who came home from school one day to find out her mother was gone, and there was nothing she could do about it.

Joanna became the woman who hunted monsters, and she couldn't afford to give that girl too much room. Had anything changed now that she could leave the monsters to someone else?

"You are not really thinking that hard about whether to get a new top?" Rue commented, and she realized she'd been holding on to and staring at the simple blue t-shirt for what must have been minutes. Joanna put it back on the shelf.

"No," she said. "I've been thinking about monsters."

"This is different. This guy seems to have fallen in with some bad people. Not that he deserves to be murdered," Rue added quickly.

Joanna didn't need any further explanation. Without blaming the victim, it was obvious that Dillon had put his own life in danger. The victims of Short and Decker hadn't done anything like that, yet there were still people who shamed them online.

"You're right. Let's go get a coffee somewhere?"

When they sat down in a coffee shop, Joanna admitted, "I'm going around in circles. I don't want to talk to Dad again, but I'm afraid he's the only one who can tell me whether Mary is making things up, or if she has reasons to worry."

"I'm surprised you'd take his word over hers."

Joanna was surprised, too, but she had an explanation.

"The devil I know? He didn't always lie to me. When he told me to never come to him for any kind of help until I was ready to give up homosexuality, he was serious. And he stuck to that."

True, it was odd that she'd give credit to anything Lawrence Mitchell said.

"It's a wild goose chase, and I'm getting nowhere. Let's get ready to go home. I'm sure after everything Denise will give us some time off to finalize the wedding plans."

"We could go see him if you want. Just to tie up those loose ends."

"I'm not sure we'll achieve that, or that anyone is telling me the truth, but...Thank you."

If anything, it would banish the nagging idea that her father could be anything worse than unrelentingly prejudiced.

꧁꧂

It didn't surprise Joanna that Lawrence didn't make time for her easily.

"You can come by Friday afternoon, but I don't have long. Renée and I have work to do."

She knew that more than work connected her father and the conservative lobbyist. That was none of her business.

"We'll go back home soon. I'd just like to talk to you one more time."

"I assume you met Mary. I don't know what else we have to talk about..." He sighed. "Don't make me regret this."

"Don't worry. It will be the last time I'll bother you with this."

She ended the call, shaking her head. Somehow, it was always about him. She couldn't let it get to her.

Why would the idea of this conversation make her nervous to begin with? She had survived far worse. Perhaps it was the sum of those experiences that had steadily worn her down. She had to remember that Rue was still wrestling with her own demons.

"Okay, Friday afternoon it is. And tomorrow, we'll see Vanessa and Theo."

"We'll still have a bit of time to ourselves."

"Which we should spend organizing our return..." Joanna paused when Rue embraced her from behind. "Booking flights." Her breath caught when Rue's hands started to wander. "Sending a message...to Denise. Okay, maybe all of this could wait a little longer."

"I was hoping you'd say that," Rue whispered, and she could forget about it all for a little while.

❦

When they arrived at the restaurant, Theo wasn't there yet. Vanessa sat in a booth by the window. While the place wasn't cheap, she was as usual fashionably overdressed.

"Theo is running late," she said. "They are still working over-time with—you know. Sorry."

"No need to be sorry," Joanna told her. "It's been bizarre, but we're almost ready to go home. This wasn't great, but it really has nothing to do with us."

"Yeah, a pretty strange coincidence," Vanessa agreed, her tone uncharacteristically somber. "It doesn't need to ruin our evening, right? Let's get started on the cocktails."

Rue cast her an amused glance. "Sure, let's do it. We could all use some lightening up."

"I thought we did that earlier," Joanna whispered to her, enjoying that her words got Rue flustered.

"Stop that. It's not fair when you do that around people who have no time to be romantic." Vanessa waved to the waitress. "Three Mai Tais please."

"Okay, what's going on?"

"A lot. Too much. I need a bit of a break from it all, and I'm pretty sure you could too."

"No kidding," Joanna said. "Anything specific we should be aware of?"

Vanessa shook her head. "Nothing you should be worrying about. Except if it's the general state of the world, it's something we should all be worried about. But you of all people deserve a time-out. For a few years, or forever." She shrugged. "Don't listen to me, it's just been a tiring week...year. I was looking forward to this," she gestured towards the waitress arriving with a tray of colorful cocktails.

"They look great," Joanna agreed. She took a sip, wondering if everyone around her was acting strange, or if her perception was far off. She had loved her time-out with Rue, hiding away in the hotel room, only emerging for a late breakfast...She couldn't help thinking that Vanessa had a whole lot more on her mind than a nice and relaxed dinner with friends. But Vanessa would talk to her when she was ready, not a minute sooner.

"So, what are your plans now?" Vanessa changed the subject. "I know you want to go back to the island, but you'll have a whole lot more options now that your record is clear."

"We are pretty happy with our lives there," Joanna said. "I don't see us making any big changes." She had thought that spending time in the city might make a difference, but here, she could never change the feeling of being an outcast—from her parents' home, from the career she'd once been passionate about. On the island, both she and Rue had jobs that paid for a roof over their heads and enabled them to have something beyond. It was where Rue had her training and her therapy. No, they weren't looking for a change. "And of course, we would never have that if it wasn't for you. Thank you."

Outside the restaurant, she saw Theo get out of his car and walk towards the entrance in brisk steps. Once back home, it would be easier to turn off all the questions. They'd be able to breathe again, this time, without needing to stay under the radar.

"It's no big deal," Vanessa said. "I'm glad I could help, and it all turned out well for you in the end." Despite her odd behavior, Joanna believed her. This was a subject where they had cleared the air between them and made peace—despite the fact that it was Vanessa's investigation that had led to her prison sentence.

"Hey. I'm sorry I'm late—"

Theo never got to finish his sentence when another car pulled up, two wheels on the sidewalk, and the next moment a bullet shattered the window.

Screams ensued as everyone ducked for cover.

It was the moment Joanna realized the rapidly growing stain on Vanessa's dress.

"Vanessa!" She took off her own cardigan and pressed the fabric against the wound. Theo looked in shock, but he was already on the phone calling an ambulance. Rue cowered under the table, her hands over her head, but to Joanna's relief, she seemed unharmed otherwise. "You'll be okay. Help is on the way."

Her lips were moving, but Joanna couldn't hear her.

"Don't speak. Whatever it is, we can talk about it later."

Theo gripped her hand and took over putting pressure on the wound. He leaned in, and Joanna had to back away to make room. When Vanessa tried to speak again, she thought she'd heard the word, "stalker." And then, "Mary."

As they heard the sirens in the distance, Joanna pulled Rue close to her. She was alarmed at the feel of blood on her arms until Rue exclaimed, eyes wide with shock,

"You're bleeding!"

# Chapter Five

R ue couldn't even begin to fathom what this meant, a random incident, someone targeting them? Targeting Vanessa? She knew she had a few minor cuts from shards flying, but she swatted helpful hands away, pointing them to Joanna. They were still at the restaurant that seemed to get more crowded by the minute.

"Don't worry. I'm okay," Joanna insisted. "We'll be okay." Her calm tone cut through the all-encompassing panic, though Rue wasn't entirely sure if the statement itself was true.

Blood was oozing through the bandage someone had provided Joanna with, where a bigger shard had embedded itself in her arm. Rue couldn't help staring, mesmerized and terrified. Too much blood. *Again.*

"Rue. Let's go to the hospital?"

Of course. She'd zoned out for a moment. It wasn't about either of them, but Vanessa. Coming out of what felt like a trance, she finally got to her feet, taking in people with frightened expressions, huddled together in groups. Police officers all over the place, Detective Allison Kato standing in a corner with what seemed to be the owner.

"Come with me?"

Rue tore her gaze away from the blood and shards on the floor and followed Joanna towards the entrance.

"You two," Allison said curtly. "Ambulance. I'll see you at the hospital."

"I can drive," Joanna said. "I swear. We just want to make sure Vanessa's okay."

"That's what we all want, preferably with no more injuries, okay? You look like you're about to keel over. Now's not a good time to argue with me."

Rue stood, listening to the words until they lost all meaning, and reality started to fade away.

She thought that Allison was going to get her wish, then the world turned black.

It was something oddly familiar, a nightmare scenario striking out of the blue. Fortunately, Rue had recovered quickly after her fainting episode, and they were both able to stay and wait for news on Vanessa.

Joanna didn't want to disturb Theo at this moment, though the questions had multiplied. What did Vanessa mean, and why was it so important for Joanna to know? Someone had been stalking Vanessa? Mary? Was it all connected?

It had to be, she reasoned. It couldn't be just Joanna's bad luck that this was the second time someone had been shot at in her vicinity in such a short time. She shuddered. Dillon had been a PI looking into Mary. Vanessa had done jobs far outside the books to help Joanna and Rue.

She cast a look at Rue who sat with her back straight, staring straight ahead. If anyone didn't need to see any more blood and chaos, it was her.

Joanna sat next to her, touching her arm lightly.

Rue flinched. "Do you need anything?"

"Me, no. I was wondering if you wanted to get something to eat. We might be here a while."

"I don't think I could eat anything. A coffee maybe. I'll come with you." Rue was on her feet quickly enough that Joanna feared she might get dizzy and faint again.

"Easy. I'm not going anywhere without you."

Rue gave her a grateful, if pained smile.

They found a vending machine from which they purchased a couple of coffees. On the way back to the waiting room, Allison Kato caught up with them.

"Any word?"

Joanna shook her head. "She'll be okay," she said anyway, not for the first time that night. She had to be. If Joanna focused all of her energy on that thought, she might be able not to think about what could have happened, with Rue sitting just on the other side of the table.

"Let's pray she will be. You're sure you didn't see anything?"

"Theo had just arrived that moment. We were talking. I'm really sorry. The car pulled up, and then the window exploded. Dark blue van, I didn't get the license plate."

It was more than that, Joanna felt guilty. For a big part of her life, increased vigilance, looking over her shoulder all the time, had come easily to her. It had only been a short time that the monsters were gone from their lives, or they'd thought so...She had let her guard down.

"We didn't know if he was going to fire again." Even that sounded unconvincing to her, though Allison nodded.

"Thank you. I'm glad you're all right. I'm going to see Theo."

"Allison, wait a minute. Vanessa, she said something to me, about Mary, and a stalker."

"She was probably in a lot of pain. We'll talk later."

She might have let her guard down, but Joanna's instincts were still sharp enough to realize when someone was lying to her.

"Allison, cut the bullshit. She's my friend too."

After hesitating for a few seconds, Allison turned with a sigh. "So silly of me to assume you wouldn't find out anyway. You understand that the pardon doesn't mean you're back on the payroll, right?"

"I'm not asking to get paid. I want someone to tell me the damn truth." Beside her, Rue stood silently.

"The truth? I don't know if that's a good idea at this point. You should talk to your mother."

"I'm here now. Anything that concerns my mother—or my father, for that matter, you can tell me. My friend was just shot right in front of me. I'm tired of all the lies."

"I really need to see Theo. If you must know, we looked into the stalker story, and it's gotten us nowhere. The story changes depending on who you ask, chocolates and flowers sent a couple of times. Mary says it was over a period of years, but your father had a different take. He thought she was making it up to gain attention. And that's a whole lot more than I should have told you. Excuse me now?"

She turned and headed for the waiting room, leaving Joanna struggling as she tried to come up with something to say. Maybe that was what she'd feared all along—that Lawrence could be right, and Mary was making things up. She certainly had sounded like that on the phone, but the woman she'd met at the show, and more recently, seemed clear-minded. Who was telling the truth? To whose advantage would it be muddying the waters?

Her money would always be on Lawrence, but now the detectives thought it too that Mary might have imagined things. A stalker.

Vanessa's words, and the context in which she had spoken them, were disturbingly real. Mary. Stalker. Now she was fighting for her life.

Did Vanessa know something Allison didn't? Was that why she'd been in such a strange mood?

"Let's go back," Rue reminded her, her hand gentle on Joanna's back. "We can try to sort out everything else later."

They found Theo talking to the surgeon. The doctor had news for them, wrapped in standard phrases, but good news. To her surprise, Joanna found herself wrapped in a tight embrace a moment later. She could feel her eyes well up.

"It's okay," Rue whispered.

It wasn't okay. People she cared for still got hurt around her. Joanna was afraid it might never end.

We stayed until Theo all but kicked them out of the waiting room. Joanna could understand wanting a bit of private time, so she didn't protest. He wouldn't be on the case, but she knew he and Allison would communicate.

Allison. Her words still resonated with Joanna. She was a good cop who wouldn't take accusations lightly, especially when it was about a woman who might be in danger. Lawrence didn't have a lot of respect for people who weren't like him, and he let it show. Allison would see through his bigotry, which meant—what? He had told the truth about Mary?

Joanna didn't want that to be the case, though she had to admit the evidence was adding up.

Much later than anticipated, she and Rue finally got to bed.

"To think that this was supposed to be the fun part of the week," she said, her attempt at dark humor failing miserably.

Rue held her close, keeping the fear at bay that everything was going to fall apart once more.

They went to check on Vanessa in the morning. Rue was aware that Joanna would have liked to ask her about her comment. Given the fact that Allison and Theo were present, she opted to postpone. Rue kept a smile in place she hoped was reassuring, though it was clear Vanessa wasn't up to many visitors or an interrogation. She was still heavily medicated, fading in and out.

Was there nowhere safe?

The idea that they could return home and go back to the quiet, blessedly uneventful lives they'd lived for some time, seemed to fade further and further away, like a dream she could barely remember anymore. That was selfish, of course.

Vanessa had put her career on the line for the both of them. The least they could do was to stay until they knew she'd be okay.

Rue wasn't looking forward to seeing Lawrence Mitchell either, but she had promised Joanna to be by her side, and she wasn't going to break that promise. They needed to be able to rely on each other to survive this—wherever "this" might take them.

The closer they got to leaving, the quieter Joanna got, and that was nothing new either.

Rue wasn't sure if it was a comfort to her that this might be the last time they had to deal with him. Her former boss had no interest in coming to the wedding, and he acted like every contact with his daughter was inconveniencing him.

The housekeeper opened the door to them and led them into the den, where a woman in her late forties got up to greet them.

Rue knew her, Renée Madison, a conservative lobbyist whom Lawrence had been dating when Rue was still working for him.

"Rue, it's so good to see you again," Renée said with a polite smile. She went on to shake Joanna's hand. "You too, Joanna." She stopped after that which was probably better for anyone involved.

Lawrence was the consummate cliché, a rich businessman who, after a failed marriage, turned to a woman barely older than his daughter. Rue might have been romantic enough to think it could be true love, if she hadn't gotten to know him up close and personal. But this wasn't about her. She was only here to support Joanna.

"Could I offer you a drink? Lawrence was held up at the office, but he'll be here in less than half an hour. I can ask housekeeping, but I make a pretty good Martini myself."

"Yes, sure," Rue heard herself say while Joanna declined at the same time. "No thanks."

Renée turned to the bar and started fixing cocktails. So, she lived here now. That was no surprise either.

She cast a glance at Joanna who was probably having similar thoughts. Rue understood that she wanted to stay clear-headed for difficult conversations ahead. Rue didn't have any point to make. She knew that both Lawrence and Renée had invested considerable effort in discriminating against people like her and Joanna. The least she could do was drink their expensive liquor.

Or perhaps she was frantically doing whatever she could not to think about the exploding window, shards of glass, and blood everywhere.

⚯

Lawrence Mitchell returned fifty minutes after the time they had scheduled. He didn't apologize, not that Joanna had expected anything of the kind. He sighed dramatically, cast a glance at Rue and Renée who were halfway through their second Martini, and said,

"I think we should discuss this in private."

For once, Joanna agreed. "Thank you for meeting me," she said as she got up, aware that Rue cast her a slightly panicked look. If the situation hadn't been as dark and disturbing as it was, Joanna might have found it amusing. Once upon a time, it had been part of Rue's job to be polite around people who didn't respect their very existence. Rue no longer held that job, and she was lightly blitzed.

She had better make this quick. Lawrence took her to his home office, where he sat behind the desk. He didn't offer her a seat. Joanna preferred to stand.

"All right," she said without preamble. "Help me put this together. You always told me that Mom didn't want to be with us, that she left because she chose a fantasy career over her family."

"Yes, and how many more times I need to tell you? She had a decent voice. A producer who wanted to have sex with her told her she could become a star, and she went for it. I really don't know how else I can make you understand."

Joanna gritted her teeth. She regretted not having a drink.

"Why were you still giving her money? And what about that stalker, did you know about him?"

He shook his head, exasperated. "Two different things. You're wasting your time with this, and mine, I might add. I give her money because I'm not the monster you two think I am. As long as she's doing her thing, she's happy and functional. That's all we could ever ask."

"What the hell does that mean?"

"No need to swear. It means we both agreed she shouldn't be around you. Of course, that was before I knew that Mary was fairly harmless in comparison. Look at you, implicated once again in a murder and attempted murder. Does it ever stop with you?"

"I don't know where you got that, but I'm not implicated in anything. Her crew member had gambling problems, and one of my friends was shot yesterday." She stopped, reminding herself there was no point in arguing with him, ever.

"Not the first time this kind of thing has happened, has it? Regardless. You asked about the stalker. In the first couple of years, Mary performed in front of twenty people or so. I sent some chocolates so she wouldn't go off the rails, that's all. She made up a bigger story, and the people around her didn't call her out on it."

"So, she didn't make it all up—isn't that what you told the police?"

"I told them the truth. Like you said, this has nothing to do with the man who was killed. Maybe your friend also owed money to the wrong people."

"You don't know her." If anything, Joanna was learning the same lesson again. He didn't listen to her, never had, because her concerns didn't matter to him. Never had. "None of this makes any sense. Mary isn't sick."

For sure, she seemed to have a thriving career and a dedicated following.

"You think you can judge that after meeting her twice? I had to go on business trips often. Sometimes she just wandered away in the middle of the night. Someday you might be mature enough to thank me for saving your life."

It didn't surprise her that Lawrence and Mary were telling dramatically differing stories...Joanna was beginning to think that she might need to find someone who had been a witness at the time.

"If you really want to know the truth, go to Dr. Hollister. He is retired now but still lives in town." He opened a drawer and leafed through some papers before handing her a business card. "I hope you'll leave us alone after that."

# Chapter Six

Terry Dillon, crew member for a cover band. Terry Dillon, PI. Allison had gone back to poring over the contents of the dead man's electronic devices, only now there was even more of an urgency to get results.

Theo was still in the hospital with Vanessa. Questioning other patrons of the restaurant had proved to be useless. They had been so traumatized no one could give a better description of the van or its driver.

Who had hired Dillon to look into Mary, and how had that turned into a years-long-employment with her? The lab was still working on what seemed to be his work-related files, all encrypted. He was deeply in the red, but no hints yet as to whose patience might have come to an end as they waited for the money.

She scrolled through some of the pictures, intrigued to see a clean-shaven Dillon shaking hands with businessmen and local politicians—that was about twenty years ago. He got his license shortly thereafter and started working for Mary only a few months after that, his appearance drastically altered.

Allison sat back, taking in the contrast.

Lawrence Mitchell had assured her that his ex-wife was "hysterical" and that there had never been a stalker.

What if Terry Dillon had been the stalker?

He walked alongside the wall, amused at the thought that the police had probably put up a board, trying to make sense of the riddle somehow. He loved that they were all in the dark, the investigators, the people who thought they could control him.

Those who had no idea he was coming for them, one by one.

Joanna had not imagined she'd spend her last days in the city chasing ghosts, but here she was, trying to find a person who could help her separate lies from the truth. She was doing a search on Dr. Hollister. Given the experiences she'd had with her father, the way he'd given up that information so easily was raising red flags with her.

Nevertheless, what she could unearth about him online wasn't a surprise to her or Rue. He seemed to run in the same circles, hold the same beliefs, and donate to the same politicians.

Joanna closed the laptop, aware that Rue was studying her curiously.

"It's maddening," she said. "The more I learn, the less I know. It's all filtered through being mad at her, because she left me behind...but she was very young when all of this happened. I'm still not sure it did because she was troubled, or flaky, or they put a lot of pressure on her."

"Maybe I'm biased, but I'm inclined to think it was the latter," Rue admitted. "You know Lawrence, of course. I've seen him do business in recent years. I think that if they had an argument, he'd kick her out just for the point of winning. Because he could."

"But he didn't kick her out. He got her medical help, as it seems, and put money into her career."

It was hard to imagine that they'd been all wrong about him, and that Mary would still come out as the bad—worse?—person in this. At least, Joanna had those childhood memories of Mary playing with her and singing to her. She'd been focused and present. What happened? When did those "troubles" start?

"Like you said, she was very young. Let's face it. Women could end up in a psychiatrist's office just because someone with influence said so. And we know he considers everyone and everything he doesn't agree with, "deviant." Rue sat in her chair with a frustrated sigh. "How did I ever stay in that office so long?"

"You had to pay the bills." There was a time when Joanna had felt less forgiving about this fact, but they were long past that. Something was still bothering her, beyond what happened to Vanessa, and someone close to Mary.

Lawrence had been secretive all this time, and now...He put her in touch with Mary, and that doctor, why? What was it that he wanted her to see? Why be this subtle when he had never held back opinions?

"I was lucky I was already eighteen when he found out I was a lesbian. The worst thing he could do was to stop paying for tuition." Only a few months' difference, and Joanna might have been faced with problems much graver than how to pay for staying in college. Even decades later, the thought was chilling. "To think that kids today still go through this makes me sick. I will call him, and then we can put this aside for a bit. I hope. How about we go see Vanessa and get dinner afterwards?"

"Sure, let's do that."

They hit a somewhat lucky streak: A receptionist put Joanna through to Dr. Hollister. It turned out he had already spoken to Lawrence and expected her call.

"He was a doting husband," he recalled. "So sad that Mary wasn't able to see that. Of course I'll meet you."

By the time she ended the conversation, Joanna wasn't sure if she should laugh or cry. His blind spot was obvious, but he might still have valuable information for them.

When they arrived at the hospital twenty minutes later, they found Vanessa alone, and a lot more lucid than the other day.

"I had to kick Theo out for a bit," she said. "Allison promised she'll get some food into him."

"That's good. I'm glad you—" Joanna found herself choking up all of a sudden.

"Yeah, at this point it looks like we're indestructible, right? But...fuck, this really hurts whenever the meds wear off a little."

"I can imagine."

"For Christ's sake, Joanna, don't cry. I don't want to go there, not yet, okay? I know you're not sitting on your hands. There was something I wanted to tell you before we were so rudely interrupted."

"About Mary's stalker."

Vanessa nodded. "Allison and Theo aren't sure how serious this is, but given the fact that I'm in this bed, I'd say it's pretty damn serious. There must be a connection. It looks like Mary was trying to get away, from him, from it all, but some powerful people kept an eye on her."

For a moment, Joanna wondered if that was still the pain meds talking.

"You left IA shortly after you arranged relocation for me and Rue. That guy who got me to the island, your contact? He's done this before. And so have you."

She was fishing, but Vanessa's resigned expression told her she was on to something.

"I can't tell you much more, but that's about the gist of it. It wasn't that easy to make you disappear, it was impossible with Mary. I guess that runs in the family."

Joanna pulled herself a chair, to sit closer, and also because she needed to sit.

"Am I supposed to understand any of this? Because I don't."

"If I was you, I'd have a couple of dinners, maybe catch one more show, and let that be it. You don't need to know everything. Sometimes that's better, Joanna."

"Lawrence gave me the number of a doctor that treated Mary back in the day. We're going to see him tomorrow."

"And find out what? Joanna, I know you never listen when someone tells you to leave it be. This time, you should. Not just because it could get you into trouble, but a whole lot of other people as well."

"You?"

"I'm tired."

"I need to know if she is in danger, or if it's all her imagination."

"What do you think the good doctor is going to tell you?"

Joanna didn't think she needed to answer that.

"Terry Dillon is dead. The doctors in this hospital took a bullet out of my body. That part is not imagination. But it's not your job."

She was right. Joanna had a hard time listening when it came to that.

Dr. Richard Hollister lived in a house not unlike Lawrence's, the furniture and décor blatantly displaying wealth as Joanna had expected.

"I understand you have some questions," he said after they sat in the spacious living room. "I talked to both Lawrence and Mary, and they assured me I can give you any information you might need." He was in his late seventies maybe, with a neatly trimmed white beard and an immaculate haircut.

"You spoke to my mother?" Joanna asked. She wasn't even sure whether to be surprised—or whether he was telling the truth.

"Oh yes, we keep in touch still. She has made great strides since I first met her."

"How did you meet her?"

He held her gaze as he spoke. "This might be hard to hear, but Lawrence tells me you were a police officer. You've probably seen much worse. See, Mary wanted all the comforts of marrying an older man, but the reality of it was difficult for her. Lawrence, of course, was in love, so he overlooked the warning signs."

"Like what?"

"She was home alone a great deal of the time, and she was already prone to paranoia. It was easy for someone to come in and tell her Lawrence didn't have her best interests at heart. She had affairs, and unfortunately, she was never able to take responsibility for anything, until much later."

Joanna hadn't missed the fact that he had eagerly jumped right into a conversation that might constitute breaking patient/doctor confidentiality, unless Mary had really agreed to him revealing all those details.

"When was that?"

"Not long after you were born. By the time they sought help, things were really bad, and she had regularly brought men to the house. Lawrence feared for your safety, and hers, and so he had to make a hard decision."

"To get her committed because she was cheating on him? And you went along with that?"

"No, there were other problems to consider. I can assure you, it was urgent. After that time, Mary and Lawrence found a solution that worked for both of them."

It hadn't worked for her, ever, though Joanna didn't think the doctor would understand.

"I hope this will help you find peace. I understand you've been through difficult times yourself." Hollister was Lawrence's friend, so it wasn't clear if he meant the fact that she'd had to kill a man, twice, or something entirely different.

"Thank you. I'm fine."

"I don't practice anymore, but there are a lot of good people in this field. We were able to keep Mary on a good path. There is help for you too, even at your age."

She couldn't help but laugh at that. "I should have known something was wrong when my father was so eager to get me to see a psychiatrist. No thanks. I'm getting married soon."

"If you ever change your mind, I could give you a list of colleagues that deal with this very kind of thing."

With an incredulous laugh, Joanna got up to leave, Rue following her. There was nothing more to learn here.

❦

"Can you believe this guy? 'Even at your age.' What the hell is wrong with him?"

"Too many things to name." Rue leaned in for a surprisingly passionate kiss when they were in the car. Or perhaps it wasn't surprising at all. Something good had to come out of this meddling of sad, petty men.

Mary had a life. Joanna did. Regardless of people who thought that for wanting just that, something about them needed to be fixed. She was almost ashamed at ever having doubts about Mary's state of mind. The story still had too many holes, but given what she knew, Mary had reason to be cautious to the point of paranoid. It ran in the family, maybe. It might also have to do with knowing Lawrence Mitchell.

"Let's go home," she said. "Do something that would have gotten us into a psych ward."

Rue leaned back into her seat, her face flushed with excitement.

"I like the sound of that."

Long after Rue had fallen asleep that night, Joanna sat up, wrestling once again with the thoughts that continued to plague her no matter who they were talking to. Half-truths, flat-out lies, much of it wrapped in bigotry and prejudice.

She used to be better at identifying those and catching the other side in a contradiction—as a cop, as an inmate doing what it took to survive.

She had found some of Mary's songs on the internet, someone who had put up snippets from a show. It never ceased to amaze her that this treasure trove of information had been out there for this long.

Maybe she had been ignorant. Maybe, and that was disturbing to admit, she was more like Lawrence, because he had been the parent who'd been longest in her life. Jaded, expecting the worst of people. That might be why she was so torn between the varying versions of the story. She thought she could tap into that time when Mary was around, loving, reliable, but instead she was a grown woman who had accumulated experiences of disappointment and betrayal. That did sound like Lawrence, expect some of the betrayal was imaginary in his case.

Joanna wasn't gay just to spite him.

But if Mary had cheated on him for real?

With headphones, as not to wake Rue, she listened to the haunting tunes in the dark, with her cell phone's screen the only light. The quality wasn't stellar, but it was enough to convey the emotion, to hit her. It was much of what she hadn't allowed herself to feel, since, for the longest time, she'd felt her life could only go one way.

She could have a real life now, a future, with Rue by her side, back at home...Real, and stable, perhaps she still wasn't sure what to do with that. Sometimes, when they made love, she'd still cling to her as if it might be the last chance before they had to go separate ways again.

After all the time they'd spent together, Joanna was more than ever aware that someone staying, with her, in her life, was still a fragile concept.

⁓

At first, she thought the sharp knock on the door was for the guests next door, even though it sounded alarmingly close. Joanna took off the headphones the moment a voice yelled, "Police! Open the door!"

"It must be a mistake," she said to Rue who was wide awake, her expression shell-shocked. "I'm coming!" Joanna quickly put on her robe and tied the belt around her waist before she went to open the door. Within seconds, she went from her quiet nighttime activity back into the nightmare.

"What the hell are you doing? What are you doing?"

Rue's angry voice sounded like it came from far away, or under water. So did the other voices,

"Joanna Mitchell? You need to come with us."

"Why? What happened?"

"I'm Detective Masters." She turned to the man in the long coat who was flashing his badge in her face. "Dr. Richard Hollister was found dead. We believe he was murdered."

"Am I under arrest?"

"For now, we'd like to follow us to the station, just to talk. We know you were at his house today."

"This is ridiculous," Rue intervened. "We have nothing to do with this. You can't make her!"

"Not yet, but it would be better for you if you cooperated." Masters was talking to Joanna. "You could take your chances, but the next time, I'll come back with a warrant."

She knew by heart what came next. Even if she wanted to, Joanna wasn't sure she'd be able to form words at this moment.

She was sure that the murderer knew a lot more than any of them did, about what Lawrence and Hollister had done, about Mary's story. Eventually they'd unravel all these ties.

"Can I just put on some clothes? I swear I won't try to run. There's no window in that bathroom."

One officer went inside to check, and, obviously satisfied with what he'd seen, he nodded. She couldn't afford to be drawn into the past. This was nothing like it. Joanna hurried to put on underwear, socks, jeans and a sweater, her motions quick and mechanic. She needed to think. Reality was fleeting, the situation triggering memories, drawing her all the way back to the time Vanessa Young had knocked on her door, accompanied by two uniformed officers.

"I'm not sure how I can help you," she said when she returned to the room.

"Let's talk about this downtown," Masters said.

"Just a second, please. Rue, don't worry. We'll clear this up."

"What do I do?" Rue asked in panic.

"Take a deep breath. Call Theo, and I'll deal with the rest."

"Ma'am," the detective reminded her. "Ms. Carmichael, we might need to talk to you as well. Don't leave town."

Two murders, one shooting in her immediate vicinity. She would have brought herself in.

# Chapter Seven

H er mind was spinning. It all came down to the can of worms she'd opened just because she wanted to have a conversation with her mother in the present. Joanna didn't think she'd be in this interrogation room for long, though part of her wondered if this had been unavoidable. People looked at her, treated her differently when they learned she'd killed a murderer.

Only Rue had never treated her differently.

She couldn't afford to get distracted.

The detective returned to the room, carrying a cup of coffee.

"Can I get you anything?" he asked.

She almost smiled. Joanna knew every tactic in the book. He'd try to soften her up, get her to talk. This man was obviously underestimating her.

"No, I'd prefer we'd get this over with quickly. I don't need a lawyer. Rue and I met with Dr. Hollister earlier today. He was very much alive when we left."

"Why did you meet him?"

"He's a retired psychiatrist as you know. He treated my mother a long time ago. According to what he said, my parents had both given him consent to share some of her medical history with me."

"Isn't that unusual?"

"Well, he's the doctor. I was under the impression that he knew what he was doing."

"Were you angry at him?"

"No. Why would I be? I wanted to know more about my mother. My father gave me Dr. Hollister's number, and he agreed to talk to us. We didn't learn much, but that's not a reason to kill someone."

"What is a good reason to kill someone, Joanna?"

"Excuse me?" she said, starting to get irritated with his approach. They couldn't have anything on her, except Joanna's and Rue's prints in the house. They were probably the last ones to see him alive, save for the killer, and someone had seen them leave.

"If they hurt women, that would be a reason, right? Because you care, and you've killed a predator, a serial killer. No, wait, that makes two."

"Wow. You studied up on me. I'd be impressed, except that's all easy to find. If you know who these men were and what they did, you already know that Hollister was nothing like that."

"What about if you think someone hurt women? If you thought he hurt your mother, would that have been a reason for you?"

Joanna sat back, dumbfounded for a moment.

"Now you sound like one of those conspiracy theorists with a blog and a social media account. Hollister was a doctor. He treated my mother. I didn't lay a hand on him."

"You were questioned as a witness in the Terry Dillon murder, is that right?"

"Oh, come on. I didn't know the man. We were about to leave the concert venue when we heard a scream. We only went back to find my mother and make sure she was okay. You might want to check with Detective Kato."

"And just a few days ago, former IA Inspector Vanessa Young was shot literally sitting across the table from you."

"Vanessa is my friend!" She made no more effort to hide her exasperation. "Why would I want to get her killed? That makes no sense. I see what you're looking at, two people dead, and one in the hospital. My name comes up each time, so that's not something you can ignore. But I swear the pattern you're looking for is elsewhere. Someone is looking to hurt Mary. I've heard from several people that she had a long-time stalker. You find him, you'll likely solve those murders."

The detective drank from his cup, a wry smile playing over his lips. "Well, thank you for your help, Ms. Mitchell. That's indeed an interesting alternative theory. But perhaps the pattern I'm looking at is you trying to get back at people who hurt you, and your mother, and, by proxy, abusers at large."

Joanna shook her head.

"You tell me you didn't know Dr. Hollister had a history of committing young women whenever their husbands wanted to keep them in line?"

Joanna sat up straighter.

"No, I didn't know that. All the information I had was what little he and my father told me."

"You didn't think they might have treated her unfairly?"

She didn't know how to answer that question.

"Terry Dillon, PI undercover as band crew member, had been in court for domestic violence a couple of times, went to prison when he violated several restraining orders."

"That's news to me too, and I'm sure Mary wasn't aware."

"Ms. Young stopped you in your tracks when you had just found your vocation to rid the world of evil."

"You're still wrong."

"Am I? Why are you still here, Joanna?"

"I'm not sure what you're asking."

"You have a life somewhere else, don't you? The governor pardoned you. You could have just packed your bags and go back home, but you decided to stay. To tie up lose ends?"

"I wouldn't have that life if it wasn't for Vanessa. I owe her. I'd never hurt her!"

"Okay. Why don't we take a break?" he suggested. "Still nothing I can get you?"

"If this means you'll want to go around in circles some more, yes, I want a coffee. I didn't kill anyone or have anyone killed."

"All right."

"Milk and sugar please."

After he'd left, she sank back into the chair, exhausted. Of course, there were cameras, but she didn't want to show any weakness while he was still in the room.

The worst of it all? His theory made sense to some extent. She'd never thought about hurting Vanessa. But she could never turn away from abuse either. Perhaps, for a split second, it had felt good to end the lives of a couple of sadistic killers.

⁂

"Relax, take a breath. I'll make some calls, and this will go away, I promise you." Theo's calm reaction was a relief. At the same time, Rue felt angry that anyone could be calm about this big scary mess.

"Will you get back to me right away?"

"Of course. Don't worry. We'll figure this out."

"Why would they think they can arrest her? We were in the doctor's house, we talked, and we left."

She hated that Theo paused for a few seconds.

"Let me get on this. I'll call you as soon as I know more."

After they'd ended the call, Rue, already dressed, picked up her coat and purse and left the hotel room. At the reception desk, she asked the concierge to call her a cab.

She was lucky in all of this, privileged that there was somewhere she could go in the middle of the night, scared out of her mind.

Her father opened the door to her, looking worried. He was dressed in a robe over PJs. Rue had prepared what she was going to say, but all she could do was stumble into his embrace, crying as she struggled to explain what had happened.

Not only could she come here at this time of night and be welcomed. Her parents were a steady supportive presence in her life, and they had never judged her for being in love with a complicated woman.

While she was aware that likely neither of them was to blame for the immediate chaos they'd been thrown into, once more, Rue was angry at Mary and Lawrence Mitchell, because they never cared to provide Joanna with the same safety.

"Thank you," she whispered.

⁓

She might be in denial, or Joanna simply hadn't come to terms with the gravity of her situation yet. They hadn't touched knives, or anything that could be constituted as a weapon in Hollister's house. Joanna had left her gun back on the island when Theo asked them to come to the city.

Why was she still here?

The detective had informed her that her lawyer was on the way before he left her. Even that didn't strike her as unusual. Rue would have contacted Theo by now, he and Vanessa knew whom to call. This would all be over in a matter of hours.

Wouldn't it?

She leaned back in her chair, covering a yawn with her hand. It had been a while already, and she struggled to find a semi-comfortable position in the hard chair.

This incident was one more sign to guide her into the right direction. Rue didn't need this. Joanna didn't need this. She'd have to say goodbye to Mary and stop chasing ghosts. She'd also have to lean a bit harder on Vanessa to inquire what she'd meant about those powerful men watching Mary, make sure she was safe.

Then they could finally go home. Get married. It had become a faraway, almost unreachable dream. If they weren't careful, it might slip out of reach altogether.

She sat up straighter when the door opened, suppressing a relieved sigh when Theo walked in. Joanna's relief didn't last long. She saw his concerned expression, and she didn't like it.

"The lawyer's here."

"Lawyer? What lawyer?"

"Vanessa pulled some strings, and that's all you need to know. Listen to me, you do what she says, no straying from the script. This is important."

"Okay. Thank you. Believe me, I want to get this over with as soon as possible. But this is all just a formality, right? My dad told us to see Dr Hollister."

Theo was the one to sigh.

"I wish this wasn't the one time you listened to him. Governor O'Neal had your back that last time, because frankly, we all should have. This is different."

"I'm aware. What the hell are you saying? I didn't kill the guy. Yes, he probably locked up my mother when he had no grounds except that Lawrence told him to—"

"Joanna, stop. This is serious. As I said, this lawyer will help you get things straightened out, but you have to do as she says.

This is a courtesy from Detective Masters. I shouldn't even be in this room."

"Theo, wait. What do they have—or think they have?"

"I can't talk right now. I'll see you later."

She'd tried to do the right thing, and now people thought of her as some self-appointed avenger. It couldn't be farther from the truth.

She longed for peace so much.

⁂

"Later" turned out to be early the next morning, but at least Theo had good news: Joanna could go home.

"What did you tell them?" The private attorney Vanessa had sent appeared competent to her, but even so, this was soon. What kind of network had Vanessa cultivated over time?

"Don't look a gift horse in the mouth, that's what I'm telling you. I'm serious. Go home...There are people waiting for you on this other side of this door."

Masters was unhappy, she could tell, but he let her and Theo pass and leave the room. Exhausted beyond measure, Joanna stumbled along the hallway after Theo, and through a couple of double doors into a waiting area.

Seeing an equally tired-looking Rue immediately lifted her spirits. She let herself be drawn into a close embrace.

"Hey, can I borrow her for a second?" This was a happy surprise. Rue had not only thought of getting Theo involved, but she had also contacted an old friend of Joanna's.

Kira wrapped her into a firm hug even as she chided, "What did I tell you about staying out of trouble?"

⁂

She would have liked to have a hot shower and crawl into bed, stay there for the foreseeable future until it was time to go home. Joanna was aware she couldn't do it, with everyone around her still expecting explanations. She wasn't sure she had any.

She was most grateful for Rue and Kira—as much as she managed to still keep herself upright, something inside felt brittle, about to snap.

"I think Theo will want to have a word," Rue said, "but he's agreed to meet at the hotel. We all go, you can change, and we have breakfast?"

Her stomach was still tied up in knots, her body slow to catch up to the good news.

"I think that would be a good idea."

"Take your time." Kira laid a gentle hand on her back. "We'll all be here."

"I know. It's so good to see you. I wish it wasn't in these surroundings."

"Same here," Kira agreed with a wry smile. "But you made it. Rue said you have an amazing buffet at the hotel that I'm really curious about."

"It is pretty good. All right, let's all get out of here."

# Chapter Eight

"Trust me?" Rue said. They had gone up to their room while Kira was waiting for them in the hotel lobby. "I know you're exhausted. I am too."

"It's fine. I'm really glad to see Kira."

"Good. I'll wait here for you."

Before Joanna headed for the shower, Rue pulled her close.

"Hey. I'll be just in there for a few minutes."

"I know. It's silly, right? I wasn't the one they interrogated, but...this was the first time in a long time we spent most of the night apart. I hated that."

"Yeah, me too." Joanna said. She kissed the top of Rue's head and then gently disengaged herself from the embrace. "You can go to the breakfast room with Kira. I'll hurry up."

"Are you sure you'll be okay?"

"Absolutely."

Her body was still in fight or flight mode, which Joanna didn't mind. It kept the breakdown away for the moment. She didn't yet have the time or the safe space to indulge in it.

Someone was murdering people in her vicinity, and showing her that if it wasn't for influential friends she was lucky to have, she could go down for those crimes. Those murders—and one attempted—had started when she began asking questions. About Mary. About the stalker.

It wasn't a surprise that Lawrence would dismiss a woman's fears about a man crossing lines, but why would he pretend it had been him?

She dressed quickly, and then went down to the breakfast room where Rue and Kira sat in a booth, together with—

"Mom!"

"I'm sorry I couldn't be here earlier today," Mary said. "I'm so glad you're here. What a ridiculous idea to think you could have harmed Dr. Hollister."

"Do you have any idea who did?" Joanna asked, before she sat. She hadn't missed the flash of alarm on Mary's face.

"No, and let's not talk about this now." She reached out to take Joanna's hand. "I know I disappointed you so many times, but I hope now that you have tickets to go home, we can just spend the morning together?"

"Let's make a toast," Kira suggested. "To unbreakable women."

It wasn't until then that Joanna realized there were four mimosas on the table. She'd be the first wanting to escape reality for a little while. Across the table, she caught Rue's apologetic glance, and she realized that the words "Trust me" had encompassed more than this little gathering.

Tickets.

"I can do that," she said, raising her glass.

The brittle feeling inside didn't go away.

❧

Rue watched Joanna and Mary standing at the buffet, relieved that Joanna's body language was more relaxed than earlier. She couldn't let her out of her sight either.

"Don't worry, you did the right thing," Kira assured her. "She has a hard time putting herself first, so every once in a while, someone else has to do it for her."

"I'm selfish, too," Rue admitted. "I never wanted to come here in the first place, but Joanna had no choice. So, I'm here. We didn't know that she'd get to meet her mother."

"And that too, seemed to have gone better than expected."

"In some ways." Rue sighed and took another sip of her mimosa. The second one. "If you don't count the dead bodies. It's like we're cursed or something."

"Listen to me, Rue," Kira said firmly. "No one's cursed. All of us had some serious crap happen to us, but we're not cursed. We're survivors."

"I guess you're right." Rue realized she was choking up. She wasn't going to spoil the perfect celebration. The tears she'd cried at her parents' house had to be enough.

"I know I am. I wish you'd enjoy the city a little bit more, but I'm happy for you, and the life you've built. You two of all people, deserve it."

"Let's hope Joanna is as ready to go back to it as I am."

⟨⟩

"You and I both know this is all connected somehow. Dad told me where to find you, and he pointed me towards Dr. Hollister. Now Hollister and your crew member are dead, and a friend of mine's in the hospital. I just want to make sure you're safe."

"You heard what your other friend said. We're unbreakable."

"This is no joke, Mom. Hollister told me you and Dad gave him consent to talk about your medical history."

"He said that?" Mary laughed. It didn't sound happy. "Not that it's a surprise."

"They clearly didn't have your best interests in mind. Why didn't you sever all ties with him? You did with me."

Somewhere in there lay the key to something more sinister than she might have imagined before. Or she was losing it.

"I love you. I've always loved you, and it breaks my heart that you have plenty of reasons to doubt me. But that's the truth. I would have taken you with me if there had been any chance."

"What made you think there wasn't? Lawrence certainly didn't have use for a child."

The regret in Mary's expression was genuine. Still, her explanation didn't make much sense—or did it?

"He didn't want me around you. He was willing to go to great lengths to make sure of that."

"Because you cheated on him?"

"I did, once," Mary said without hesitation. "I was young, naïve, and stupid, thinking this could give me any kind of leverage...and perhaps I believed it too, that if I stayed, you'd be tainted. That were was something about me that needed to be contained."

In some strange way, Joanna could sympathize.

"But it's all over. Dr. Hollister is gone, may he pay for his sins wherever he is now. You and I both have a life. Don't worry about me. I can take care of myself."

"I still have friends with the police. They could—"

"No, Joanna. I'll be all right. And I know, with Rue by your side, you will be too."

"The stalker..."

"Whoever he is, he kept his distance for many years. I don't think anything will change."

"I hate leaving you alone." Her censors were down. Mimosas might be the reason, or the night she'd spent at the police station. Mary didn't comment, or perhaps she was wondering if Joanna had a better understanding of her dilemma now.

"Joanna. Can I talk to you for a minute?"

She turned around to see Theo standing in front of her.

"If you let me eat, yes. I haven't had the chance to try any of this yet."

She watched as Mary picked up her plate and went back to their table.

"Okay, what do you need from me? And by the way, thank you for helping me out."

"I wish I could take the credit," Theo said. "Vanessa directed all of this from her hospital bed."

Of course she did.

Unbreakable women. There was some truth to that.

⁂

"Rue tells me you're going home."

Apparently.

"Is there a problem with that?" Her nonchalant tone easily belied the abyss of fear that came with the question. He couldn't know. Joanna hadn't known until the moment she said it out loud.

"No, not with you traveling. You're free to go wherever you want."

"But?"

"Isn't there something that's bothering you? I mean I understand you're tired of it all, but there are still a lot of questions regarding your mother."

"Tell me about it. There are plenty that she and Lawrence don't want to answer. I can't force them."

"True."

She followed his gaze to the table where Rue, Mary, and Kira were engaged in a conversation.

"You know something I don't."

"I'm not sure," he admitted. "Allison has been working on this more. I've tried to spend time with Vanessa."

"That's understandable. I'm sure you've been trying to figure out how those incidents were connected."

"Your mother got married young. She got overwhelmed, there was talk of affairs, Lawrence wouldn't have it. I'm right so far?"

"Unfortunately."

"You thought she had left, but instead, your father involved Dr. Hollister. He got her committed and threatened her in case she wouldn't do as he said—leave you with him and continue her career, but under his watch."

"Sounds like the controlling bastard he is," Joanna said dryly.

"Did she tell you about the band member who died under mysterious circumstances? That was before she left your father."

"Yeah, so, it was a long time ago. People die." She managed a fairly calm tone despite the blow his words delivered. People seemed to have died often around Mary. She wasn't sure if she could deal with this at the moment, fatigue setting in full force. And new worries. She could feel herself tremble. She needed to sleep, without nightmares.

"Don't you think it's strange that so many of these deaths seem related to Mary somehow?" Theo, predictably, asked.

Joanna shook her head as if she could make the implication go away. "I think we're all getting ahead of ourselves. It's been hell with Grace and her boyfriend on the run. For all of us. Let's not mix up things, shall we?" The uncomfortable realization was starting to set in: Theo wasn't just coming here on a hunch.

"Do you trust her?"

"That's a big word. Whatever the circumstances, she did run out on me when I was ten years old. She might have had a reason. I still trust her more than Lawrence, why?"

"The crew member, the psychiatrist, and a band member."

"You think there are more? That's ridiculous. Mary might have made mistakes. I'll be the first to admit that, but she's not a killer."

"I know there are more," he said. "And I don't think she is, but she might not have told you the whole truth either."

"So, you think that she knows something? That she's scared of someone? There is a lot of talk about that stalker, but every time I try to get to the bottom of it..."

"Someone else gets hurt," he finished grimly. "I know you'd like to put all of this, your life here, behind you, but I keep coming back to your family."

"I don't know what to tell you, Theo. Have you asked Vanessa?"

"Forget about it. She doesn't know anything."

"She knew about the stalker."

Theo's expression told her he was as frustrated as she was.

He asked the million-dollar question: "Why, in all this time, has no one tried to find that stalker if everyone knew about him?"

Because Lawrence Mitchell had told them it was a hoax, Joanna answered in her mind. Did she have to look at her father in a different light?

⁂

Mary had made sure that Lawrence wouldn't be there when she came to the house. His presence still had the same effect on her it had since a short time after their wedding—she felt trapped, like she couldn't breathe. Perhaps this was a futile mission, but she had to try.

Joanna and her wife-to-be would leave in a few days. They'd be safe. Vanessa Young had her own people to look after her.

There was still someone else she was worried about. Even if that person didn't give a damn.

Renée Madison regarded her with the same pitying expression she had reserved for women who didn't agree with her. So, most women. But Mary hadn't come here for a political discourse.

"What do you want? Lawrence isn't here."

Behind the less than polite tone, there was still a hint of concern, that one day, Mary would want Lawrence back, and that he'd take her. Women like Renée would never admit it, but they didn't trust the men in their lives.

"Good. I just need a few minutes with you. What I'm about to tell you won't be easy to hear, and you might not believe me, but I need to make sure you understand what you're in for."

"What I'm in for? Get a grip, Mary. I'm sorry things didn't work out for you. He's with me now. We're happy."

"That's what I thought, a long time ago. All I'm telling you is to get out while you can. Things might seem fine at the moment, but he will find a way to destroy your career and life if you're not careful."

"You base that on what, your own inability to stay faithful to a man who gave you everything? If you're talking about Dr. Hollister, I know the story. You were out of control, a danger to your child. I realize you told her the same lies."

"It's not too late for you," Mary insisted.

"I don't have to listen to you."

"Lawrence is not who you think he is."

"Funny. You're everything he said you were. Crazy."

"Did he do you a huge favor, made sure you owe him? He will come to collect, I swear, and it won't be pretty."

She could tell from the flash of panic on Renée's face that she had found the pressure point. But then the fear was gone, and the other woman regarded her with the same condescending expression.

"If you don't leave, I'm going to call the police. Haven't you had enough of that yet? Maybe they'll lock you in an institution again."

"If you stay with him, there's no saying where you're going to end up. Renée. You know I'm right."

"Are you threatening me? You leave my house right now."

"I'm not threatening you. I want to help."

Mary hesitated for a split second, before she pulled the card out of her pocket.

"Don't share this with anyone, please. But if you ever need help, call this number."

"You're ridiculous, Mary. Good night."

Mary turned and left without another word. The car was waiting for her. She had done everything she could, but she feared it wouldn't be enough.

# Chapter Nine

"I hope you're not mad at me." Rue's tone was soft, like her touch on Joanna's naked back. They had lost track of time, evasion, sweet distraction, until they couldn't avoid that conversation any longer.

"For bringing guests and making me go out for brunch? No. I'm beginning to understand that there are some answers I'll never get from Mary. And it was nice to see Kira again."

"So, you'll be good with going home this weekend?"

"I'll be good to go wherever you are."

Her content sigh was muffled by the pillow as Rue leaned over and kissed her neck.

No need for any more complications.

It was only mid-afternoon, but they had slipped into a light sleep...

*"Come on, we need to get going."*

*Joanna didn't want to go anywhere, and she didn't like the frightened tone in her mother's voice, the tight grip on her wrist. Where would they go anyway? All her books, clothes, and toys were here. Mary all but dragged her down the stairs and to the front door where they both jumped when Lawrence Mitchell stepped into their way.*

*"You're not going anywhere," he said.*

*Joanna recognized the tone, the one where it was pointless to argue.*

*"Let us go. I'm not going to tell anyone. I just want—"*

*"Want what, Mary? Be normal? That's never going to happen."*

*"I know things," she said, clutching Joanna's hand tightly enough for her to yelp.*

*"I could have you locked up in the loony bin for the rest of your life."*

Joanna bolted upright, gasping for air. Slowly, she oriented herself in the present, realizing she'd woken Rue. Her concerned gaze spoke volumes.

Usually, they could trace the source of night terrors to a handful of predators, all of them dead. This was different. Joanna didn't know if it was Mary's story that had prompted the dream, or her own memory. If it was the latter, how could she have forgotten about it for so long?

Shivering all of a sudden, she pulled the sheet around her.

"Maybe she was telling the truth. Maybe she tried to leave with me, and he stopped her. If that's true...I owe her an apology."

Rue put her arms around Joanna.

"She still left you with him."

"Maybe she thought she'd be in a better position if she was free, than committed to a psychiatric hospital by her powerful husband. Wow. I knew he wasn't a good guy, but the more I find out about him, the worse it gets. To think she never really got away from him...it's depressing."

"She's still accepting money. That's her choice."

"I know...Do you think there's a chance we could still have her at the wedding?"

"I'm okay with it if you are."

Joanna hadn't known until she said it out loud how important this was to her, and not just because she knew it would make Lawrence angry.

He'd been going down the list, past and present. Hollister had been easy. Men like him always were, because they thought of themselves as invincible, and they expected everyone to bow to them. A traditionally trained psychiatrist teaming up with a successful businessman, young Mary Mitchell didn't stand a chance.

But there was no use in the stories of the past coming out, when she had a life now, when she could soon have a life with him. They had both waited for so long. There were only a few names left on the list, including the woman he had to keep from stirring it all up. Nothing and no one would stand in their way.

No one was going to save Mary but him.

He wasn't going to share.

"Your ex-wife was here earlier today."

Lawrence Mitchell wasn't always generous with his attention. Renée knew it, and she was used to it. Even now, she wondered if he had heard her, but the next moment, he put his drink aside and turned his gaze on her.

"What did she want?"

"Oh, you know Mary. Nothing of importance."

His gaze softened. "I'm sorry you got dragged into all of this. Whenever my daughter is in town, she creates a circus, and this time, Mary is a part of it. It will all be over soon."

"It's not important. I'm fine."

"What exactly did she say?"

Why was she on edge all of a sudden? It wasn't like she believed a former hippie who had never grown up or contributed to society much. Lawrence didn't have much respect for Mary or their daughter. He had a point, didn't he? That was what he, what they believed. Mary couldn't be trusted. She lived in her own reality. Wasn't that the truth?

"Some ramblings about how I'm not going to be happy with you in the long run. It was pitiful, really."

"If she comes around again when I'm not here, call me. I don't want you in any danger."

"From Mary?" She gave a surprised laugh that, Renée realized, sounded slightly off. This conversation was almost as bizarre as the one she'd had with Mary. And Mary was the crazy, paranoid, vengeful one.

"We need to be careful, that's all. I wouldn't want anything to happen to you, and as you've seen, people get hurt around her."

"If she contacts me again, I'll let you know," Renée promised. "What would you like for dinner?"

"Renée, I haven't finished my drink yet," he said. "I'll let you know when I'm hungry."

<hr />

They went to visit Vanessa who was, against medical advice and to Theo's chagrin, resting at home. Afterwards, Joanna went back to the basic internet search she'd done on Mary before. Most of it was recent, about the cover band, the concert at the Colosseum and the murder that had happened there.

She found a few video channels with uploads of recent performances. *MaryRocks. MaryKilledMeSoftly.* She flinched at the latter. Most of the comments came from people who had attended one of the concerts, and they were mostly positive, or backhanded compliments, like *pretty good voice for her age. Still looks good.* Because looks and age were always the first things that people noticed, and that mattered to them about a woman. She made a frustrated sound and picked up her wine glass. Instead of going down to the restaurant, they had bought a few snacks after seeing Vanessa.

*I went to college with Mary, and she's always been amazing.*

*Too old for my taste.*

*Hey, you idiot, get off my channel.*

The more she read, the more grateful Joanna was that she'd never found the time to develop much of an online presence.

*Too bad. She could have had a great career if she hadn't become the second wife of a jerk almost twice her age.*

Wait. What did that mean? She couldn't be talking about Lawrence?

"If that's true, I'm one hell of a lousy cop," she said out loud, and Rue gave her an amused look. Rue had been a lot more relaxed since it was decided, and they had a date for their flight home.

"Is it a good time to remind you?"

"That I'm not a cop? I'm aware, thanks, but come look at this."

"It's trolls on the Internet. I wouldn't give much weight to that. There were some people who thought Short and Lester were the original Bonnie and Clyde."

"Yes, but..." Joanna opened the channel of the woman who had made those baffling claims—if that picture was her. She had always assumed, and never questioned, that her parents' marriage had been the first for both Mary and Lawrence. Then again, he was much older, so it wasn't completely far-fetched that he could have been married before? She shook her head.

"Why am I surprised? It's not like anyone ever told me the truth, about anything. For all I know, I should ask for a DNA test."

"You should be planning your wedding," Rue reminded her.

"I can do both. I'd feel better if Mary could come with us. Maybe she'd be more open with the distance."

When Joanna looked up from the screen, she was relieved to find Rue's expression pensive, without sympathy or pity.

"Theo had some concerns about her safety too."

"Then the police should make sure she's safe. I'm not sure how I feel about bringing all of this to the island...not Mary," she corrected herself quickly. "She's your mom, of course she's welcome. But perhaps she's right to say that you should leave the past in the past. It's not like Decker...or any of them."

Joanna cast another look at the screen.

*That's some MILF.*

*Leave her alone, bastard.*

*What's it to you?*

*You're going to find out.*

She closed the page. "Let's look at dresses," she said.

❦

Joanna couldn't let go of the idea, especially when they were about to enter their own marriage. It all fit together. For Lawrence Mitchell, marriage was between a man and a woman only. That didn't mean there had to be only one woman, or that love was any consideration. Did Mary know? Did Renée Madison know? The woman, online troll or real person with some knowledge about events long gone, how did they find that information, and were they a friend to Mary? She could accept the fact that she was no longer a cop. It wasn't her job to solve the murders, and the fact that she had barely escaped going to jail for one of them, should tell her everything she needed to know.

But this was her family history. She deserved to know, especially after Mary and Lawrence had stalled her at every turn.

It was late. She didn't care.

Lawrence didn't pick up the phone after eight rings, so she tried again. And a third time.

"For Christ's sake, you're as crazy as your mother. Do I need a restraining order for both of you?"

It was a chilling thought that he might have friends in high enough places to make it happen.

"I don't think so, but you tell me. Were you married before you met Mary? Do I have siblings?"

"Are you on drugs?" he asked irritably. "That's none of your business."

He hadn't said no.

"You're my father."

"That doesn't entitle you to any of this. God, can't you see you're embarrassing yourself?"

That tone, and choice of words, still struck a nerve.

"I'm going to find out either way. Those are public records."

"Knock yourself out. My first wife died. I met Mary two years after. Are you satisfied now?"

"How did she die?" She might as well go there.

"It was a tragic accident. Now leave me alone, or I will consider that restraining order."

"Thank you," she said. "Good night."

He scoffed. Joanna ended the call and opened the computer again. With a sigh, Rue poured another glass for both of them.

Anna-Louise Mitchell, thirty-two, had been drinking after an argument with her husband, wandered around in the backyard where she fell and drowned in the small pond on the property. It sounded like a creepy Gothic novel, where the new heroine would come in and solve the murder.

"Joanna. Please. I know you're not mad, but you're going to make yourself. Stop this."

"How could I not know this?"

"Why would you, if nobody told you? You had enough on your plate, with your mom gone, and your dad being an insensitive...individual," Rue chose the term carefully. "It was wrong, what they both did, but you became the amazing woman you are anyway. You already rose beyond all this. Why can't you leave it alone?"

This wasn't the first time anyone had asked her this question. It wasn't the first time Rue had asked her the question, and it never took Joanna long to find an answer.

"I should have done something sooner." They both knew she wasn't talking about Mary, or Lawrence's late wife, any longer. "It feels like I failed...all over again."

"But you didn't. Mila, Vanessa, Allison—me. We're alive. You are. And I love you."

One day, that would have to be enough, or she'd live the rest of her life in crippling doubt. Being with Rue, waking up to the sound of the ocean every day, a routine keeping the nightmares at a bearable distance...It had to be enough. She'd been given so much more than she could have ever expected.

The phone rang.

"Theo? It's good that you called. I think there's something you need to consider." The thought had been vague before, but with the information revealed about Anna-Louise Mitchell, it was getting clearer, the possible implications harder to ignore.

Perhaps the stalker wasn't just connected to Mary. What if Lawrence was the central figure, and Anna-Louise's death was no accident? A jealous lover, a business rival, someone who held a grudge for a long time and chose the women to get back at Lawrence? There were still holes in that theory, but, as everyone reminded her, she wasn't a cop, not anymore.

"Joanna. There's something I need to tell you." He sounded serious, though not as though for her to assume something happened to Vanessa. No, he'd be...different.

"My father's first wife died under mysterious circumstances. I think that all leads back to that stalker story. It would be like him, to keep it under wraps because of his reputation."

"Please, stop for a second. Has Mary contacted you?"

"No, why?"

"Look, all hell is breaking loose here. She had an appointment with her manager this morning. It's in his agenda."

Joanna immediately understood there was no reason for Theo to know all this. Except...

"Is she okay?"

"We don't know, to be honest. We found him dead in his office. The secretary called us. She didn't see Mary, or anyone, but Joanna, this is serious. We can't reach your mother."

"With the body count, I'd say it's serious. I still think someone is trying to get back at Lawrence. He's bound to have done some shady business dealings over the years. Or someone was jealous. It always leads back to him!"

"We don't know that yet."

"You've met Mary," she said, incredulous. Joanna felt beyond weary. "You don't think she had anything to do with that?"

"I don't know what to think, except I never thought you would...It seems like a lot of men have taken advantage of her over time."

"Right. If every woman killed because of that, there would be few men left."

"I don't have time to discuss this now, but either way, it's important that we find her. She's too close to all of this."

Joanna could only agree. "I'll let you know if she calls me," she said, though she doubted she'd be high on Mary's list. Come to think of it, the atmosphere at the brunch had felt much like goodbye. Again.

# Chapter Ten

S he called the number Mary had given her, not much surprised to find the number was out of service.

"What the hell is going on?" she said out loud. "I don't believe that she all of a sudden starts to kill people who have done her wrong. She made some mistakes, maybe, but not like that. I had the impression she liked the guy."

"We're unlikely to find out until the weekend," Rue gently reminded her. "Unless..."

"I can't wait another twenty-five years. If Mary's gone, that's because she wanted to."

Even as she said it out loud, Joanna was aware she sounded uncertain.

"I hate to say it, but we've been spending a lot of money, even the part that was not helping the police find Lester. Perhaps she needed some time to herself, maybe she never even went to see her manager. In that case, she might contact you again, and you can invite her. If not...She left you before. I know she had her reasons. The same might be true now."

"Someone has been targeting Mary all along, or they have been targeting Lawrence. If the latter is true..."

Rue's eyes widened. "You think they'll go after Renée next?"

"At this point, I'm not ruling anything out. I'd hate to go see Lawrence again, but I don't know if I can avoid it."

"Maybe you can. Somewhere between those Martinis, she gave me her number and told me not to bother a busy man again."

"That's perfect. Let's at least warn her."

To Joanna's surprise, Rue caught Renée on the phone right away. Rue held the phone out to her. "You tell her?"

"I'm busy," Renée Madison said without preamble. "If this is about Mary missing, the police were here already. Lawrence is at work, I'm working from home today, and we have no idea where she is. We're good?"

"Ms. Madison, hear me out please. We have reason to believe that you might be in danger."

The other woman laughed. "Like mother, like daughter. It's frankly pathetic. Sorry to be so blunt, but I don't know how to say it any other way. Lawrence is a good man. I understand neither of you is able to see that, but I'd prefer it if you left us alone. I'm not going to leave him."

"I wasn't going to tell you that. Lawrence's first wife died. Mary is missing. All I'm saying is that you need to be careful."

"I'm starting to think you need to be in a padded cell. Isn't that true, you consider yourself to be some avenger for the women of the world? Your father lost his first wife in a tragic accident. I'm aware of that. Your mother is a flake, and you...Just stop this. Don't come around, don't call me or Lawrence. We're sick and tired of your drama."

She didn't give Joanna a chance to answer.

"Wow," Rue who had heard every word, said. "I guess we've done our due diligence here? I'm sorry."

"Don't be. You're right. I still want to raise the idea with Theo, but I guess this is it for us. I can't wait to be home. I swear we're done with the drama."

Rue smiled. "It sounds so much better when you say it. And don't believe her. She's wrong on everything."

Joanna shrugged. "Actually, I hope I am too, in this, anyway. I want her to wake up and get the hell out. I don't want anything to happen to her."

She picked up her phone and sent Theo a text.

"Where were we on those dresses?"

Renée Madison had little patience for women she thought blamed every misfortune in their lives on men—Mary, Joanna, even her girlfriend who'd had a cushy job with Lawrence's firm and one day decided she should be flaunting her lifestyle instead. With Joanna of all people.

Weak, pathetic, those were the words that she'd learned early on, and she'd spent all her life trying to prove she wasn't any of those things. She didn't complain, didn't ask for special rights, and she'd made her way into a top position in a male-dominated field anyway. Unlike Joanna, she knew when to draw the line. She hated them for sowing doubts in her mind, about more than her relationship with Lawrence.

This was ridiculous. They didn't care about her, or if she was in danger. Joanna Mitchell just needed to put herself at the center of every story. Renée couldn't wait until she and Rue had gone back to the island, Mary would go back to her happy life, more as a never-was than a has-been, and they could all move on.

She knew Lawrence would be holed up in his office until the late evening, so she'd likely have to have dinner alone. She got up to go downstairs, in the mood for a snack. Lawrence liked her for her discipline in everything, so she rarely indulged herself when he was home—but this wasn't any other day. She had earned a freaking cupcake.

Downstairs in the kitchen, she brewed herself a latte first and took a plate out of the cabinet.

She wasn't sure when she sensed a presence behind her, and even when she did, it didn't make sense to her. She was supposed to be alone in the house.

Renée saw his reflection in the glass of the cabinet, a shadow dressed in black. She thought of the gun she kept upstairs, but the next moment every thought and hope were drowned out by excruciating pain and the scent of singed flesh, the hardwood floor the only thing in her vision. And none of this made sense either.

❧

They were going to miss that damn plane. As they were browsing websites of bridal shops once more, every sound from the hallway seeming to startle Joanna, Rue knew that much for sure. The island would fade further from her mind. They might never be able to leave.

*She was going to miss the plane and wake up nearly naked in a psychopath's attic...*

No. Rue became aware that she was well on her way to sliding into a flashback. She had learned strategies to keep them at bay, and they mostly worked, but it had been a while since she'd seen Dr. Shepherd. Or had a training session with Zach.

As much as she liked being able to see her parents more often while she and Joanna were here, she was starting to feel as antsy and scared as she had before Vanessa had made her a once in a lifetime offer, to be with Joanna.

If it wasn't for Joanna, she would have never left the city. Now, because they couldn't seem to solve the complicated riddles of the past, they seemed to be stuck here for the foreseeable future.

"Joanna," she said.

"Yeah, I heard what you said about spending money. Those are a bit pricey, but it's just for inspiration. We're going to find something we like on the island."

*Are we?* She almost asked.

"I need to go home."

"And we will, this weekend. I promise you."

"I'm not okay." Rue almost regretted her words when she saw Joanna's face fall. She knew she needed to be honest. "I want to support you most of all, but I can't when I feel like everything is falling apart. I'm having nightmares, and you do too. I need to see Dr. Shepherd. I guess I could find a gym around here, but—"

"You won't have to." To her relief, Joanna didn't sound like she'd caught her off guard. "I know a lot of things haven't gone as planned here. We have a life elsewhere. I promise you we'll get on that plane this Sunday. As soon as we've settled in, we're going to set a date, and buy dresses." With a wistful smile, she added, "Ones that we can afford."

Bit by bit, Rue felt the tension that had gripped her fall away.

"I might have exaggerated a little. We have decent salaries, and part of our stay here is already paid."

"I love you," Joanna said. "You are more important to me than anyone else."

❧

Theo didn't get back to them, and a quick call to Vanessa revealed that she didn't know anything else. Rue had started to fold a few clothes and put them into a suitcase when a sharp knock startled them. Joanna was by the door in a heartbeat. If she had felt safer in this hotel room, in this city, Rue might have thought it was kind of sexy. As it was, she was once more terrified. The last time this happened, the police had come for Joanna. What now?

"I know you're in there, now open the damn door!"

Joanna rolled her eyes, and Rue sighed in relief. This was one problem they could handle.

"Give me a good reason," Joanna said. "You and Renée have told me not to talk to you again. Since you're so important. I got the message."

"For Christ's sake, Joanna."

Rue watched as she opened the door, greeting her father with the words, "I don't think Jesus had anything to do with it." Taking in Lawrence Mitchell's appearance, she knew immediately that something was wrong. Whenever she'd seen him, at work, or the few times she and Joanna had visited him at home, his appearance was always immaculate. Now he wasn't wearing a tie, and the five o'clock shadow was obvious in his pale face. He looked as haggard as she'd ever seen him.

"What the hell did you say to Renée?"

"What? I told her to be careful, because this looks like someone has it in it for you. She blew me off, and perhaps I was wrong. Maybe Mary was tired of it all and left on her own."

"I should have never given you that number," he said. Even though he was standing a few feet away, Rue shrank away from the anger. "Mary is gone. Now Renée is too. It's all your fault!"

Joanna didn't budge.

"I had a right to know. And Renée can do whatever she wants, though, for what it's worth, if she left you, good on her. If she didn't, well, it's not me you should be talking to."

"You destroy everything you touch. I should have known."

"I'd like you to leave now."

"That might be the best idea." Everyone turned to Allison who had followed behind him. "Mr. Mitchell, I'd like you to come to the station and meet with my colleague, please? I'd like to talk to Joanna and Rue."

Her calm tone didn't have much of an effect on him.

"You can't tell me what to do," he raged. "Are you even qualified for this?"

Rue was almost certain that Allison Kato wanted to roll her eyes. A professional to the core, she didn't.

"Mr. Mitchell, we need to talk to you! If you please...?"

He turned on his heel and stalked away.

"Mr. Mitchell! I'd like you to meet me at the station!"

"If you insist," he said without turning around. He kept walking.

"All right," Allison said she walked inside and closed the door behind herself. "That was pleasant. On the bright side, you already know why I'm here, so we can make this quick."

"Do you have any news on Mary?" Joanna asked.

"I don't. In addition to the bodies piling up, we now have two missing women. You can imagine my boss is not happy. Hell, I'm not happy. Let's make this quick and tell me what you and Renée were talking about just a couple of hours ago?" That question was for Rue.

Before she could answer, Joanna said, "So it's true? You suspect wrongdoing?"

"He came home to find a shattered mug, coffee all over the floor, and a smear of blood."

"Damn. I had hoped she'd left him." Her casual tone belied the genuine worry. "Any leads? You're pressing Lawrence on that stalker, right? I believe he always knew he was real, and he let this thing go on no matter what happened to the women he was with."

"That's...a theory," Allison said carefully. "Rue?"

Rue almost told her that she didn't have a better one when she realized Allison was still waiting for her answer. For a moment, she been drawn back...*the cab ride...the moment she realized he wasn't going to let her go...blood on the kitchen floor...*She shook herself. She really needed that training session badly, go at the sandbag or at Zach, hard.

"Yes. I had her number from when Joanna and I went to see Lawrence. He wasn't there so she had to entertain us for a bit. Anyway..." She hesitated, searching Joanna's gaze. Joanna nodded. "We, Joanna had just come up with the idea that the stalker might be targeting Lawrence via the women he's in a relationship. We wanted to warn Renée, I don't know, just to be careful, or talk to the police. She was pretty rude, and obviously...It's too late now." Rue became aware that she was on the verge of tears.

"Did she mention anything about feeling threatened?"

"If she was, she wouldn't mention it to either of us," Joanna said with a quick look to Rue. "I talked to her, and she sneered at me. That was the gist of it. I sent a text to Theo but didn't hear back. Obviously, you guys are busy."

Allison sighed. "That's one way to put it. I guess I'll have to go and convince your dad that yes, women are allowed to work for the police these days. Any tips?"

"Don't let him get to you," Joanna said. "That's all you need to know."

# Chapter Eleven

M ary hated sitting around. It made her restless, prone to obsess over past failures and regrets. She had no choice, knowing that the ever-present nightmares had escalated in a way that went beyond her worst fears.

Regret. Having to leave Joanna behind once more. But Joanna wasn't a savvy ten-year-old anymore, she was a grown woman who had gone above and beyond to save the lives of others. Mary had to believe that she would be fine.

Renée Madison might not be. She wasn't going to blame the victim. Whatever happened, Renée had done nothing to deserve it. Mary still wished she could have convinced her during one of their earlier conversations that next to Lawrence Mitchell was no good place for any woman. One of her own failures. They added up over time, no matter what she'd done for others, for her redemption.

It always came back to the moment she agreed to that terrible compromise.

She had trusted that Lawrence wouldn't harm a child, but he had harmed Joanna all right by choosing prejudice over his own flesh and blood. So much to think about.

She hated sitting on the sidelines.

"It's been decades," she said. "What makes you think the police can get to him now?"

"It's because I know the people who are working on this," the woman answered with a smile. "I know they'll get the job done."

Mary still felt restless, but as long as she'd known her, she'd never had reason to doubt Vanessa Young. She wasn't going to start now.

⁂

Renée struggled against the nausea that came with returning consciousness. She almost expected to wake up in a dark and dirty basement or warehouse. Her actual surroundings distracted her from the urge to throw up. High ceilings. A 180-degrees view of the city. With some effort, she managed to get herself into a sitting position. The room was huge, an office space with only a desk and a chair. Whoever had brought her here had simply dumped her on the carpet, wrists and ankles tied with some sort of cable. She remembered making herself a coffee, the shadow out of nowhere...The memory made her tremble all over.

Damn Joanna Mitchell and the trouble she brought to everyone. That might not be entirely fair, but Renée didn't have the time or patience for fairness. She was scared out of her mind. Why her? She had coached Lawrence on a possible political run before they became a couple, but he played his cards close to his vest, even with her. She still didn't know that much about his business dealings. If someone wanted to get to him, or to Mary, she couldn't help them much. Would she be able to convey that?

Or were they after something else entirely? The possibilities were endless. Nausea won after all.

⁂

He wasn't going to kill her right away. He hated the idea that after all this time, Mary Mitchell might have outsmarted him...but he knew she had a bleeding heart, like her daughter. If they could save one, neither of them would be able to hide away, on an island, or wherever it was Mary had fled to.

All through her career, Renée Madison had helped politicians make it harder for women like Mary to get away from men like Lawrence Mitchell. To lobby against the marriage Mary's daughter was planning. Ironic that all this time, she'd been digging her own grave. He laughed to himself, pleased with the metaphor.

As for the moment, he still had use for her.

Renée Madison's disappearance bothered Joanna for many reasons. Most of all she was afraid it could mean that Mary had not left on her own devices after all. If she hadn't, who was behind what looked like a concerted effort?

Someone who had something over Lawrence, someone he owed? Joanna knew he wasn't going to talk to her. She had heard Rue when she said they needed to go home. She owed Rue more than anyone, and she was determined to get on that plane, come the day after tomorrow.

She might have one last shot.

"You're not going to like this," she started, and Rue gave a frustrated sigh.

"No."

"We're going home Sunday, as planned. I promised you. I just need to check something quickly."

"You're going to do that where?"

"At Mary's. I want to see if there's any clue..."

"She was on tour. It's a hotel room. Why do you think you could find anything the police didn't?"

"I don't know that I will, but that will be the last thing. It looks like Renée was taken. We can't be sure the same happened to Mary—" Joanna broke off her sentence, frustrated with her lack of ability to make herself clear. "I don't know if it will do anything, but perhaps that's the only way I get to say goodbye this time."

Rue was on her feet the next moment, understanding the urgency.

"I'll come with you."

"I'd prefer it if you didn't."

"What if your dad comes back? I have no desire to deal with him alone."

"He doesn't hate you half as much as he hates me," Joanna said wryly. "You'd be fine, but I think it's unlikely that he'll come back. Since Theo is not getting back to me, I assume he's still talking to the police. I won't be long. If you'd like, you could wait in the hotel bar?" Even as she said the words, Joanna remembered Rue had barely left the room unless she or Vanessa was with her. "Please stay here. I'll be in and out quickly. They probably have an officer there, and they can check with Theo that it's all right."

"Okay then," Rue relented. "Anything to get you on that plane the day after tomorrow."

"I can't wait to go home with you." Joanna kissed her softly, and then straightened to pick up her coat and key card. "Maybe we'll get a drink when I'm back."

❦

To her surprise, there was no uniformed officer at the hotel where Mary, her manager and band had stayed. This told Joanna two things—the police didn't believe that she had killed him, and the search for Renée Madison had taken priority. She wasn't sure how to feel about that, but certainly blood on the floor was an indicator for urgency. That, or Lawrence was pulling strings once more.

The concierge was in his early twenties, and a tad jumpy. It was hard to blame him—it was probably the first time someone had been murdered, and another person had disappeared from this hotel. The place wasn't overly expensive, but neat and cozy.

"Look, I know this is a strange request, but I need to take a look at Mary Mitchell's room."

"I'm afraid that's not possible."

"It's not a crime scene, right? She just left. I want to help." She was all ready to present some private eye persona when he said, "You're a fan? She's a nice lady. I don't want to get into trouble, and I don't want her to get into any either." There was a moment of hesitation that didn't go unnoticed with Joanna.

"Yes, I'm a fan. To be honest, there might not be much I can do, but I'd just like to see the room for a moment. Please, it would mean so much to me."

When he still hesitated, she drew a couple of bills from her wallet. He snatched them quickly and handed her the key card.

"Ten minutes, not longer."

"I won't even take that long," she promised, and took the stairs to the upper floor. A couple of minutes later she was back in the modest suite where Mary had met her once, and the likely futility of her actions came crashing down on her.

Why was she banging her head against walls? The room had probably been cleaned already. What was she hoping to find that would help her make sense of the present, and the past? She needed to go home, with Rue. Live.

Mary had lived most of her life without her. They couldn't help each other now. As for Renée Madison, she had done everything she could.

She needed to let go of that misplaced guilt, of thinking that everything revolved around her, that she alone could rid the world of evil. She needed to be with the person who loved her.

The next moment, Joanna stood still, aware of a slight change in the air. She noticed him before he knew.

When he attacked, she was ready. There was no misunderstanding the situation. The people behind Renée Madison's disappearance, maybe Mary's, had already killed multiple times. She managed to kick his ribs with her elbow which made him jump back, but he recovered before she could follow up, slamming into her hard enough her back made painful contact with the wall behind her. He was wearing non-descript black clothes, a ski-mask covering his face.

The guy at the reception desk had given her ten minutes. A lot could happen in ten minutes. They traded blows for what seemed like an eternity until he managed to wrap his hands around her neck. Joanna resisted the urge to claw at his hands and instead, mobilized every ounce of energy she had left into bringing up her booted foot. The resulting howl was most satisfying. This time she didn't hesitate for a second. With another grunt, the man fell to the floor, not quite out, but less of a threat for a moment. Still coughing, she went for his gun.

"Stay down!"

It was rather convenient that he'd brought his own zip ties. That fact told another chilling story. When he struggled against her grip, she brought down the gun against his head, and this time, he lay still. Joanna slumped back against the coffee table. This was not what she'd expected when she'd told Rue she'd go for one last quick errand, in the hope to find clues as to Mary's whereabouts.

She called Theo who, to her relief, picked up.

"I don't have time, Joanna," he said curtly. "I'm sorry."

"Theo, wait! You're going to have to make time. I'm in Mary's suite."

"What the hell are you doing there?" Joanna reasoned she had done much over the past years to earn that suspicious tone.

"You didn't return my calls. I was thinking I could...It doesn't matter. A man came in after me and attacked me."

"Jesus! Tell me what happened."

Somehow, Joanna liked suspicion better than the obvious concern for her that his tone reflected. Her throat felt tight, and not just from the chokehold.

"I'm not used to this crap anymore."

"Are you okay?"

"I think so."

"What about the guy? Is he still there? Is he...alive?" Theo asked after a moment of hesitation, and perhaps she'd earned that too.

Joanna struggled to her feet, winced, and straightened. "He'll live. He's currently down and tied with his own zip ties. Chances are he came here looking for the same thing I did, so he's either connected to the stalker, the kidnapper, or he's both in one."

"I'll be right there. Don't move."

"I can't wait to see you," she said, though her dry tone fell flat.

"Go away," Rue mumbled when she heard the knock on the door. She was sick and tired of visitors showing up unannounced, bringing more bad news. She was also worried sick for Joanna. Not that she blamed her, but there was nothing like a quick, uncomplicated errand where she was concerned. They'd both had a long streak of bad luck, and she prayed it would be over once they were back home.

"I heard that," Vanessa Young said on the other side of the door. "Sorry, but I can't. I need to talk to you and Joanna. It's urgent."

With a sigh of the long-suffering, Rue got up to open the door to her.

"I'm really grateful that you got her the lawyer, but Joanna isn't here. She went to check something out." She'd almost told Vanessa where Joanna had gone, though she wasn't sure that would be welcome. While she was beyond grateful for what Vanessa had done for them, a hint of caution remained. For the past, maybe, where Vanessa had Joanna sent to prison. Or for the present where Vanessa obviously had mysterious and influential friends.

All Rue wanted was to be home, Joanna by her side.

"Okay. That's not ideal, but I don't have much of a choice. Could you leave her a note and come with me?"

"To do what?" At this point, she was merely irritated.

"I'll explain once we're there, I promise."

"Where are we going?" She wasn't interested in playing a game of twenty questions either.

"Please, Rue. This is important. For you and Joanna. You can catch her up later."

Rue figured that in the best-case scenario, this might distract her from the ever-present worry. If she couldn't trust Vanessa, who...? It was better not to look too hard at that question.

"I guess I'll write that note then," she said.

# Chapter Twelve

J oanna had removed the man's mask. She didn't recognize him. Mid-to late thirties, brown hair, nothing much distinguishing about him.

She had also touched his neck several times to convince herself he was still breathing. She'd clenched her hand into a fist, fingernails breaking the skin, in order to convince herself she wasn't sliding back into an uncertain reality. No straying from the plan. The governor had pardoned her for a reason. She'd go back to her life with Rue, on the island, because she deserved it.

This had nothing to do with Decker. Or Short.

"Joanna, for Christ's sake, breathe!"

Theo's voice cut through the fog as the man on the floor was starting to regain consciousness.

"I'm okay," she said, unfurling her fingers and quickly pushing her hand into the back pocket of her jeans. There was blood in her palm.

"Good. I need you to be okay. I think I bought us some time with the guy downstairs. So, let's find out what we can. Hey," he addressed the man. "What were you doing here?"

"Doesn't have ID on him," Joanna said, and Theo gave her a quick glance.

"But he does have your DNA all over him, I suppose. Why are you always in the middle of these things?" Not expecting an answer, he directed his attention back to the attacker. "Hey! I asked you a question!"

The man spat out in front of him. "You're a cop? Arrest her! Crazy bitch jumped me."

"Man. That's pathetic." Her nonchalant tone belied the worry. Joanna knew he wasn't going to convince Theo, but what if he managed to turn the tables on her later on? It was his word against hers if they couldn't tie him to the women's disappearances.

"She beat me up," he insisted. "I was unconscious."

"Why were you here?" Theo repeated.

"To see Mary. I realized she was gone, then I saw *her*. I asked what she was doing here, and she started hitting me."

Joanna wasn't distracted. "Why did you bring a gun to meet my mother?" Out of the corner of his eye, she caught Theo's alarmed gaze. This could have gone wrong in so many ways.

"I have a license to carry. She hit me over the head with it."

"And I'm going to do it again if you don't stop bullshitting us."

"Joanna," Theo warned.

"I'm serious. Where is Renée Madison?"

"Who? Never heard that name."

"What did you want from Mary?"

"What do you think, bitch? I'm her boyfriend."

For a few seconds, Joanna was speechless, and she could tell Theo felt the same. Not because she believed the intruder, but because without missing a beat, he came up with this particular lie. One that fit into the old narrative that both Lawrence and Dr. Hollister had given them.

"Theo, a moment in private?"

He followed her into a corner of the suite from which they could watch the man. Joanna had held on to the gun until Theo reached out. She handed it to him.

"I'm really sorry about the secrecy," Vanessa told her as they sat in the back of the car.

"I'm not sure what you want me to say."

"I swear this will all become clear soon. You must know I'm only doing this because I trust you, and Joanna. Not many people know the whole story."

"I can't wait." Rue's sarcastic tone did nothing to discourage Vanessa, and perhaps she was more intrigued than she wanted to let on. The relationship between Joanna and Vanessa had always been a mystery to her. If after tonight, she was to gain a better understanding of it, she'd welcome the opportunity. Vanessa hadn't left her much of a choice anyway.

"This is something that matters to me, and I know it matters to you and Joanna as well." After a half-hour drive, they had arrived at their destination, a block with townhouses in what looked like a cozy, and expensive, neighborhood.

"What are we doing here?" Rue asked.

"You'll see."

Vanessa unlocked the door and they stepped into the hallway. Rue jumped when a tall blonde woman stepped out of the shadows.

"Everything's been calm here," she said, and Vanessa nodded to her. "Thanks. Security," she said to Rue. "For now, it's just a precaution, but given what happened in the past few days and weeks, it's better to be safe than sorry."

"No kidding."

She followed Vanessa into the kitchen, where Rue stopped cold at the sight of the woman sitting at the table.

"What...Why...?" She couldn't seem to form a complete sentence.

With a smile, Mary Mitchell got up to shake her hand.

"Rue, I'm glad you're here. We can finally talk."

"I don't know." Rue cast an uncertain glance from her to Vanessa, and back. "Isn't it Joanna you should be talking to? After stringing her along with varying stories?"

"I deserved that," Mary said somberly. "I want Joanna to know the truth, and eventually, she will. I promise."

⁂

"Look, whoever took Renée, they kidnapped her instead of killing her right away for a reason. He knows something, and if you get him to the station right now, he's going to get a lawyer."

"That's how it usually works, as you might recall."

"It might be too late for her."

Theo's gaze was doubtful. "What do you suggest instead? That we torture him?"

"Remind him of his options. I don't think he's the mastermind in this, but if he doesn't help us, he could be going down for all the murders, including Renée's if we don't find her soon."

Theo didn't even object to her use of "we." Joanna wasn't sure if that was a good thing.

"I suppose it's worth a shot," he said.

"Then let's do it."

Joanna cast a glance at her watch. "I should let Rue know everything's okay first."

⁂

Rue sat at the table, and Vanessa poured her a glass of wine without asking. Vanessa and Mary already had glasses in front of them.

"Should you be drinking?" Rue blurted out.

Vanessa shrugged. "Mixes well with the pain meds. Besides, we're not here to talk about me."

"I'm curious. Why are we here?"

"It's a long story," Mary said.

"Well, I have a little over twenty-four hours. Then we'll be on our way home. I suppose you're going to tell me about that stalker."

"Among other things, yes," Mary confirmed. "I fooled myself for a long time, thinking that he'd keep his distance. But then I realized all those murders were connected, and..."

"You decided to take off, leave everyone with a mess and a million questions once again. You left Joanna with him!"

For a few seconds, the silence weighed heavy. Rue knew she was treading a fine line with the woman who was about to become her mother-in-law, but she couldn't hold back any longer. She'd spent most of her life acting polite, not making waves, trying to stay in a precarious comfort zone. But for whose comfort?

"I'm sorry, you might not know that, but I worked for Lawrence. I got to know him well enough. He's cold."

"Oh, he is," Mary agreed. "I wish I'd had other options, but I couldn't see a way out. He had powerful friends on his side. I had no one."

"Like Dr. Hollister?"

"Yes, like Dr. Hollister. If Lawrence had said the word, he would have locked me up for a long time. And they came close to convincing me that Joanna would be better without me in her life. That I was an embarrassment to her."

Rue let those words sink in, shaken by what they meant, the damage caused over decades.

"She loved you. She would have been so much better off with a parent who loved her back."

"I wish I could have given that to her, but..." Mary held her gaze as she spoke. "The psych ward wasn't the worst that could have happened to me, and being raised by Lawrence's staff wasn't by far the worst that could have happened to Joanna. I knew they cared about her, and if Lawrence got what he wanted, she'd be fine."

"This sounds outlandish, no offense. None of it makes sense. How could he have this much power?"

"You said you got to know him. You tell me."

"Dr. Hollister told us you had affairs. Maybe this one time, Lawrence had a point?"

"Rue." Vanessa's tone told her in no uncertain terms that she had crossed a line.

"Make me understand then, because if I don't, I don't see how Joanna can. Why would you enter this bizarre agreement with him when you knew what he was capable of?"

"It's exactly why I did it, because I know what he's capable of. Yes, I had an affair. I was in love. I even dreamed about running away with him, and Joanna."

"What happened?"

Rue feared the answer might be everything she didn't want to hear, but she couldn't go back now. She still had no idea what Vanessa's role was in all of this.

❦

They hadn't left the hotel room yet. Joanna remained by the window while Theo crouched down next to the man whose identity they still didn't know.

"How about this? We know you're the hired goon here. You're going down anyway, but there's some leeway for you as long as we find Renée Madison alive. If we don't...That chance will be gone."

He didn't protest, but he didn't give an answer either.

"Get him to the station, then," Joanna suggested. "I'm sure the lab will find out that this is the same gun that killed Jeff, Terry Dixon, and Dr. Hollister, and it was used when Vanessa was shot. That's adding up, buddy," she addressed the man who glared at her. "But he seems to be okay with taking the fall for whoever hired him, so who are we to do him a favor?"

"I was only to deliver her. I have no idea where they took her."

"Who are they?" Joanna asked, strangely excited about the fact that she and Theo were doing an interrogation together. There was no reason to be hopeful yet. They didn't know where Renée was—or Mary.

"Some guy who wants to teach a lesson to your old man. I didn't murder anyone, okay? They just want to scare him a little, pressure him into signing some contract. That's all I know."

"How much did they pay you?" Joanna demanded.

"Two grand up front, three after the job was done. I can show you the intersection where I dropped her off. Black van. That's all I know."

"You're going to repeat all of this at the station," Theo said. "But first you're going to show us that place. Joanna?"

"I'm coming," she said, trying to make sense of everything she heard. Lawrence Mitchell was still at the center of the story—and she wasn't convinced they knew the whole truth yet.

❦

Rue looked at her cell phone as the text message was coming in. "It's Joanna," she said. "Can I tell her...?"

"I'd prefer if you waited," Vanessa said. "Tell her I took you on a girl's night out."

"She's with Theo. Apparently, they have a lead on Renée Madison. She says she'll be back soon."

"She'll wait for you."

Rue started typing, and she hit "send" before Vanessa could take the phone from her.

*Mary is safe.*

"Joanna needs to know," she defended herself.

"There are more people involved in this, on both sides. If this gets out, I don't know for how much longer we can guarantee anyone's safety." Vanessa's tone was stern.

Rue held her gaze without flinching. "I think we weren't finished here. Mary?"

"You're right. We should get to the end of the story, because I think Vanessa has more to tell you as well. I made plans to take Joanna with me. She knew Ethan, and she was comfortable around him. For a short time, I was naïve enough to think it would all work out, and Lawrence would just let us go."

*He didn't*, Rue thought, a shiver skittering down her spine.

# Chapter Thirteen

T he man by the name of Mike Plummer all of a sudden couldn't shut up.

"I work in construction," he said. "The guy who owns the company does business with Mitchell, and he knew that I was in debt. One day he calls me into his fancy office, makes me an offer I can't resist."

"Your boss wanted you to kidnap Renée Madison?"

"I couldn't turn down the money. They were going to have me fired and pin something on me."

Joanna couldn't bring herself to feel a lot of compassion yet. The man who had attacked her in the hotel room wasn't an amateur. She was sure he was used to deals like this, doing the dirty work in exchange for money or other favors. She wouldn't be surprised if the construction job was little more than a cover.

"Something, what? Like break into Lawrence's house and kidnap his girlfriend?"

"Funny," he snapped. "A guy died on a site a few weeks ago. It was drug related. But they said it would be easy to find the evidence that I did it."

"What did they want with Madison?"

"They didn't fill me in on all the details, but I figured that Grant, my boss, had it in it for Mitchell. He'd tried to buy the company or something, and they were pissed at him."

They had gone up to the location where he had handed Renée over. Minutes later, two teams of uniformed officers that Theo had requested, joined them.

"You have no idea where they were going from here?"

"None, but Grant has property and construction sites all over the city."

"You'll have to narrow it down for us," Joanna said. "Think harder."

She checked her messages, suppressing a sigh of relief when she saw Rue's. Everything was still in motion, but knowing that Rue was with Vanessa, and Mary was safe, went a long way to ease her mind.

❧

"William Grant," she said, making an effort to keep her tone light and conversational, and keeping the disgust out of it. "I knew you were desperate. I didn't expect you to go quite this low."

"It's not personal, my dear Renée. If you hadn't gotten involved with Lawrence, this could have been avoided."

"There I thought you had a thing for Mary."

He laughed. "You're smart, but not that smart. Didn't you know that all paths to Mary lead via Lawrence? And he seems to like you. I guess we're going to find out how much. I hope I didn't waste too many resources by keeping you here."

He went over to a cabinet in the corner and took out a bottle of whiskey, and two glasses.

"Why didn't I know earlier this was here?" she asked out loud.

Grant remained unfazed by her sarcasm. He poured two glasses and held out one to her.

"No thanks."

"Oh. I forgot," he said, referring to the fact that her hands were tied behind her back. "I'm so sorry." He pressed the glass against her lips hard enough for it to be painful. "Let's have a drink together, Renée, shall we?"

The taste on an empty stomach made her nauseated.

"Why am I here? Lawrence doesn't do business like that. He'll have gone to the police already."

Grant shrugged. "Let him. All he needs is a little reminder who's in charge here, and believe me, he'll get it soon." He gingerly set his glass on the floor and then slapped her. "He's keeping Mary away from me, this is what happens. Are you catching on? You should."

"I know people were murdered. Something about a stalker. Lawrence told me it was all a made-up story, but—" The realization hit her with full force. "Why get those people killed?"

He shrugged. "Because I can? I don't like it when people don't uphold their side of the bargain. I send them a message. That's all there is to it."

"You and Lawrence go way back. You *are* the stalker."

"I've been watching over her, and believe me, she needs that. She's been hanging around dubious people, and her no-good daughter, and I don't like it."

"That's not my fault. I have barely spoken to Mary or Joanna, at all."

For some reason, he seemed to find this funny.

"Oh, sweetheart, I know they tried to warn you about men like me, but that's not the point. You still don't get it. I don't care if you live or die. I'm not sure Lawrence cares, but like I said, we're going to find out. Life will go on either way, and Mary will no longer run from me."

For the first time, she was beginning to understand the depth of his delusion. Knowing the kind of privilege and resources he had, Renée felt the terror rise within her. Grant could send her back to Lawrence in pieces and still get away with it.

Perhaps Mary had done the right thing after all.

"Lawrence had found out that I'd cheated on him, but he didn't confront me right away. Instead, he had a PI follow me around for over a year. They knew Ethan and I were making plans to get away with Joanna. One night, Ethan came over. We were just having dinner." She paused as if to brace herself for the next part. "Lawrence was on a business trip, or so I thought. A man broke into our house."

Vanessa's expression was solemn. The blonde woman overseeing security stayed in the background, didn't speak much. Her lips were set in a thin line. Perhaps she, too, had heard too many stories like the one Mary was telling.

Rue had the urge to jump up and run from the room, because her imagination was running wild with the scenarios. She didn't want to hear any of them. Rue had her own reasons to be apprehensive. What made it worse—Joanna would eventually have to hear everything they said in this room.

"The man...He just stood in the living room all of a sudden. He had a gun, and he...shot Ethan."

Mary had tears in her eyes, or maybe it was Rue seeing everything through a blurry veil. "I knew he was going to hurt me too, and I was so scared he might hurt Joanna. I tried to run, he tackled me, and I somehow got hold of the gun. I pulled the trigger. The next thing I saw was Joanna in the doorway. I'll never forget the look on her face."

Rue gripped the edges of the tables with both hands as she struggled to understand, and stay in the present.

"She never talked to me about any of this."

"She might not remember."

"Lawrence was there only minutes after. He took her to her room, and when he came back, he told me he was going to clean it all up. And that I had to leave and never contact Joanna again, or she'd know I was not only crazy, but a murderer."

Rue sat back, stunned.

"He orchestrated all this, and you still left Joanna with him?"

"I know it's hard to understand, but at the time, I didn't think I had any other options. He hated me, not her. He got her a therapist, and together they made her believe it was all a bad dream. I honestly thought it was for the better."

With all the energy it took to listen to Mary's testimony, Rue didn't have any left for anger or judgment. She didn't think Joanna had forgotten, or that she was aware of it. The trauma lingered somewhere in her mind. Rue knew a thing or two about the subject, and she understood that Mary, too, had faced extensive trauma.

All because of the egos of megalomaniacal men. There was a relief in directing the anger where it belonged.

"I need to speak to Joanna. Thank you for trusting me with this, but I still don't understand what this has to do with your stalker or the murders. Or why we are here." She couldn't get that image out of her mind, Joanna, ten years old or even younger, taking in her terrified mother, and two dead men. Her stomach lurched. Other images threatened to overlay the first. "Maybe it doesn't matter. Joanna should be here. She went to the hotel room to look for you."

"Where is she now?" Vanessa asked, sharing a look with Mary.

"Still with Theo. I guess she met him there."

"I agree she should be here, and soon. It's about time we clear all of this up."

"Why now? What is different?"

"I didn't learn about any of this until a few months ago," Vanessa said. "And I think we have a way of finally stopping him."

"The stalker...or Lawrence?"

"With a little luck...both."

# Chapter Fourteen

Theo had offered to have an officer drive her back to the hotel, but Joanna declined. She was still in a strange restless mood. It would all be better once they were back on the island, and she could stop worrying about unfinished business, a job that hadn't been hers in a long time. Go back to fixing minor broken objects and find the satisfaction in knowing that there was a place for her, a life that she didn't mess up.

Someone who loved her, no matter how many times she'd messed up before.

In the cab, she gave the driver directions, telling herself that this didn't mean she was still seeking validation from Lawrence after all these years. He'd never respected her mother. When he looked at Joanna, he saw traces of the woman who had betrayed him, though these days he might see what he considered a sexual deviant as well. It didn't matter. She and Rue were going home on Sunday. This was the last chance.

"I have no time for you," he said without a greeting. Even though she'd expected something like that, Joanna flinched. "What kind of trouble did you get into...again?" She reached up to touch the bruise that had formed around her neck. "No, don't answer that. I'm about to leave."

"Can I come with you? I'm really sorry about Renée. Theo and Allison will do everything possible to find her."

"Yes, I'm relieved this is in the hands of real cops. On second thought, since she's a woman with conservative viewpoints, you don't care so much, do you?"

"I care about every woman who suffers at the hands of a predator," she snapped back before she realized that this exchange was futile. "I'm going home. I'm never going to bother you again if that's what you want, but I need the truth."

"What kind of truth would that be? You want me to go with Mary's version? I'm tired of this. I've put up with her longer than anyone would have."

"Perhaps you still love her?" It pained her to say it out loud, but any way she could reach him, might help. He scoffed.

"In any case, everything that happened in the past weeks, it's connected to Mary and the stalker. I know you've been over this with the police, but details often come back later. It could help us find Renée."

"Forget about it. I know where Renée is."

He still managed to catch her off guard.

⁂

"I have twenty-four hours. If I don't deliver Mary, and twenty-five million dollars just for the heck of it, they'll kill her."

Lawrence's tone was matter of fact—poker face or a lack of concern, Joanna didn't dare guess.

"This is ridiculous. Why didn't you tell the police?"

"Oh, come on, don't be naïve," he said, impatient. "He's got skeletons in his closet, so do I. It's in everyone's best interest to solve this without the police."

Part of her felt naïve, and stupid, because how could she have not known? Another part was still stunned at the entitlement of her father, and the other man, pushing women around as if they were nothing more than pieces on a chess board. Winning was all that counted, no matter the cost to others.

"You only know that he has her, or you know where he's keeping her?"

To her surprise, he didn't string her along waiting for an answer.

"I'm not sure about the latter, but I have my suspicion. Now tell me, where is Mary?"

"I don't know," she said quickly. "I was looking for her earlier." The seconds ticked by in heavy silence, before she realized what he'd meant. "You're not saying what I think you are? You'd be delivering your ex-wife to people who want to kill your girlfriend?"

"I'm trying not to get anyone killed here."

"So why are you telling me all of this? I'm not going to keep it a secret."

"Oh yes, that's exactly what you're going to do. You're going to help me get her out, if you give a damn."

"I need to call Detectives Randolph and Kato. I can't take the risk. The governor pardoned me, but neither of them will sign off on any of this."

"It's not my problem. I'm going to meet with William Grant in half an hour. If you feel like showing me any gratitude for everything that I've given you, you're going to help me out."

For several seconds, she was grasping for something to say. "You disowned me when I was eighteen. You want my gratitude now?"

"How about I kept you from that nut job mother of yours, paid for the best schools and your piano lessons? A roof over your head, and food on the table?"

She did her best not to shrink back from the disgust in his voice. She'd always assumed, but at this point, neither of them was holding back any longer. So be it.

"I'm so sick and tired of your bigotry, and I'm not surprised that Mom was looking for any way to get away from you. But I don't want anything to happen to Renée. Will this guy keep his word?"

"He will," Lawrence said.

Joanna reminded herself that while his promises had never been worth that much, he would follow through on a threat. Perhaps, tonight, that could work in their favor.

A strange, awkward silence settled between them as they drove. It occurred to her that in the past decades, she hadn't spent as much time with her father as she had in recent days. That wasn't necessarily a good thing, Joanna reflected. After realizing that she couldn't count on her parents, she had looked for and found family elsewhere. On the force, for a few years, though most of that family had turned its back on her too. Not for who she was, but for what she'd done. Theo and Vanessa had put a lot on the line for her.

She wouldn't forget that, ever.

"So, you're going to negotiate with him, for the life of your girlfriend, as if that's a normal business transaction."

"You wouldn't know anything about that, would you?" His tone was calm, but he gripped the steering wheel harder. "This is the grown-up world. There is no safe space." Lawrence said the term as if he'd tasted something disgusting.

"Pains me to say it, but I agree with you on the latter. You've always done that, right? Bent the rules to your advantage."

"And you're your father's daughter, aren't you? Chummy with the governor, who would have thought?"

"It was about priorities. They wanted me to help them catch a killer."

"You could do what the entire police force of the city, the state even, couldn't do? See, this is why you're my backup tonight."

"Thanks, I guess. Is it much farther? I should let Rue know that I'll be back later."

"Whatever," he said with a dismissive gesture, and Joanna hit send on the text message.

⁂

The more the evening proceeded, the more Rue felt like she'd slipped into an alternate reality. It was never a good feeling. She had gotten up and started pacing, her glass still in hand.

She was struggling to remember all the techniques she'd learned for when she was overwhelmed. Joanna's story. Her own experience as the hostage of a serial killer.

Mary Mitchell, trapped for decades, at the mercy of a man who had known and been able to twist her secrets into something to keep her from her daughter.

Rue didn't wonder any longer why Lawrence had given in so easily when Joanna had pressed him for the information. The damage was done. Mary and Joanna would never get those years back, and the story no longer held his interest.

He was with Renée Madison, who was missing.

And the stalker was still out there.

"How are you going to do this? Why you?"

"Maybe I found a place where I can put my lingering guilt to good use?" Vanessa suggested. "No, it's not just about Joanna. I know that's a touchy subject, but I did what I did because I believed it was the right thing to do. I did the job because I thought...and I still think that if cops don't follow certain rules, we all lose."

"You changed you mind?"

"No, I didn't. I left my job to invest in good people who've hit a rough patch. I wish I could have met Mary sooner. But we can change things now."

Finally, Rue sat.

"I can't believe I worked for him for so long, and I never saw anything beyond the average annoying bigoted attitudes."

"People can do a lot of damage if they have those attitudes, and the money to act on them," Vanessa reminded her.

"He kept the stalker in Mary's life, thinking he could control him. Thinking it was perfectly normal to threaten his wife with getting her committed and using his connections with other powerful men to keep her in line." Rue took a sip, and then another. "How have we not burned down everything yet?"

"There are still some good men. I'm with one," Vanessa reminded her.

"Emphasis is on some. My question stands."

***

"William is cocky," Lawrence told her. "He's not going to bring much security, and he'll rely on me doing the same. Just in case."

He surprised her once again when he opened the glove compartment to take out the handgun and laid it in her hands. "I know we haven't had the best of relationships, but I also know if anyone can help save Renée, it's you. Please."

Him using the word might have been the most shocking thing that had happened in a long time.

"This isn't good, Dad. We should still call the police."

"You were the police once. I don't trust what they've done so far, and if I recall, your own experiences weren't the best. I know how to deal with William. Let's do this."

She looked up at the tower looming in the dark. She could see beams and bare concrete. Only the lower stories had windows already.

"It's a trap."

"Not if we play this right. Look, he's had this thing for Mary for a long time. He even has some of her recordings in his office. If he thinks he'll look like the winner, he'll let it go, and we can all go home."

"You didn't tell him where Mary is?"

"How could I? I don't know."

She took another look at the skyscraper in progress. "You're sure she's here?"

"That's what he said. Let's go."

Below them, the lights of the city faded further away as they climbed flight after flight. Joanna noticed that Lawrence was in good shape for his age. He didn't slow down or stop. She thought she might have been so occupied with making sure Rue took good care of her physical and psychological needs she might have neglected her own at some point. Then again, on the island it was easy to do the job and leave all discipline aside afterwards.

She longed for the freedom they had there, the lack of scrutiny. When she arrived to fix a broken air conditioning or exchange a piece of furniture, people barely noticed her. But she couldn't think of this now, not with so many lives on the line.

They came to the nineteenth floor. It was windy, plastic panes wafting in the gusts. Joanna shivered, not because she was cold. Much depended on timing right now.

"Good evening, Lawrence."

The man who stepped out of the shadows was of average height, mid-sixties maybe, his suit probably the price of a new car. With a jovial smile, he extended his hand.

Lawrence scoffed at the greeting.

"Suit yourself. I assume you brought me what I wanted...or did you think I might be interested in someone younger?"

"William, meet my daughter Joanna."

"The killer. Interesting."

Joanna stood, unflinching even though she could hardly believe the exchange.

"We just want to bring Ms. Madison home," she said.

"You knew the conditions." William Grant ignored her, addressing Lawrence solely.

"I talked to the bank. They are initiating the transfer."

"That's nice. About Mary."

Joanna could hear muffled sounds, but as soon as she took a step forward, Grant held up a hand.

"Not so fast. If this goes sideways, poor Renée will make a long drop." Joanna halted.

"I'll tell you where Mary is, if you let Renée go. She doesn't know anything."

"Well, that's not the point, is it? But I'll show you I'm a reasonable man. Proof of life, if you will. Hey," he shouted over his shoulder. "Bring her in!" The construction tarps rustled, and a moment later, a man pushed them aside. He was dragging Renée Madison with him. She looked worse for wear, her face tear-streaked and the left side of her face sporting a bruise. Her eyes widened when she saw Joanna.

"See." Grant grinned. "That's pretty much how I found her. No harm done, right, Renée?" He reached out to pinch her cheek.

"Excuse the question, but since we're here," Joanna said. "Why Mary? What got you interested in her?"

The older man looked her up and down. "Your daughter doesn't know when to be quiet, does she?" The goon in black sent him a questioning glance, but Grant shook his head. "This is all very amusing. I'll answer your question, sweetie. It was fun for a while. I did your father a favor when he asked me to. I kept her in line. She never slept with any of those musicians again, because she knew someone was watching. But Lawrence made a promise."

"He promised you my mother?" Joanna said incredulously.

"Don't sound so indignant. I could have had her any time I wanted to, and he knew that, right, Lawrence? I just got tired of the people starting to interfere, people around her. The PI Lawrence hired. Your friend."

While thinking about what happened to Vanessa still made her blood boil, Joanna was aware that something still didn't add up. If Grant was powerful enough to orchestrate all this, she had to be missing something.

"Don't try so hard," he advised. "And frowning like this will give you wrinkles."

She almost laughed at the absurdity of the situation.

"Cut the bull, William. You might have enjoyed toying around with Mary, but most of all you wanted my business. You just weren't smart enough to build something on your own."

"Well, you don't look so smart now."

"I sent you the address," Lawrence said. "Whatever you do, don't be an idiot. She's there with Young, and my misguided former employee. I'm sorry, Joanna. Young brought her there. It's out of my hands now."

"What the hell are you saying?"

Lawrence shook hands with Grant and turned around.

"Dad! You can't walk away from this—" The man in the black clothes had pulled the trigger, Lawrence toppling to the concrete floor.

Joanna didn't waste a second.

# Chapter Fifteen

I n a heartbeat, it became crystal clear why Lawrence had brought her here, and it was not out of concern for Renée, Mary, or anyone but himself. She had only a split-second before the man turned the gun on her, but she was faster and fired a shot. Grant's minion stumbled to the ground, clutching his shoulder.

She trained the weapon Lawrence had given to her, on him and Grant. The goon's semi-automatic had skittered to the floor when the bullet hit him. Joanna kicked it out of his reach.

"Now what?" Grant asked mildly, though he did raise his hands. "My boys are waiting downstairs, and they're loyal. You want to kill me, you better jump. If they get to you first, it won't be pretty."

"I'll take my chances."

"That's a pretty big gamble. This time, the cops might lock you up for the rest of your life. The governor didn't pardon you for future crimes."

"Thanks for the lesson in my legal situation. Now get on your knees."

Carefully keeping an eye on the goon writhing on the floor, she inched closer to Renée who was shaking hard, her gaze unfocused. She wouldn't be much help, but Joanna couldn't be too picky. She prayed that Theo and Vanessa would be able to handle things on their end. She couldn't afford to get distracted.

Joanna used the Swiss Army knife she carried to cut through the cable that bound Renée's wrists.

Grant laughed at her demand. "Lady, I don't get on my knees for anyone. They'll be here in a minute. You might want to think about—"

"Shut up," she snapped. Renée flinched at the knife making contact with her skin. She started rubbing her wrists and struggled to her feet. Joanna feared that she might fall if they tried to go down the same half-finished concrete stairs. "Stay where you are for a second," she whispered to her. She kept the gun on Grant, not wanting to let on that she wasn't entirely sure what to do next. With her other hand, she took out her cell phone and called Rue.

"Joanna!" Rue had picked up right away, and she sounded worried. "Where are you?"

"Listen. You all have to leave. Lawrence gave away Mary's location. You need to go right now!"

"Okay. I'll call you back."

Grant was still highly amused, his stance much to relaxed for someone in his situation.

"Get down, or I swear I'll shoot you!"

He shook his head but complied after she fired a shot inches from his feet. Renée yelped.

Joanna saw the terror in her eyes a second before a hand wrapped itself around her ankle and pulled hard, making her stumble.

❦

"This is getting old," Vanessa grumbled when they climbed into the back of the car. The blonde woman was coming with them, and she was on the phone with someone, updating them on the situation.

Rue could feel a numbness starting to creep up on her. She was terrified, but she couldn't afford to feel all of it at this moment, the weight of the revelations, and the possibilities bearing down again.

If she allowed herself to consider them, she'd have to confront the fear that she might not see Joanna again. Rue wasn't sure if she could survive that fear another time.

She tried to brace her fall and kicked behind her, with moderate success. There was no time. Grant would try to run, or go for the gun, and she couldn't let that happen...Another kick, and the man howled as she made contact with the gunshot wound. She got free, stumbling to her feet, realizing that Grant was trying to make a run for it.

"Stop!" she yelled. "You called me a killer, Grant. You know I won't hesitate."

"I will pretend I didn't hear that. Mr. Grant, you're under arrest..."

Joanna lowered the weapon to the ground, blocking out the rest of what Theo was saying to him. She went over to Renée who was still cowering in the corner and helped her up, drawing her into a hug when she realized Renée had trouble standing upright. Or maybe it was herself, it was hard to tell.

Renée started to sob, and it wasn't until then that the full impact of what happened caught up with Joanna.

She flinched at the touch to her shoulder.

"Joanna," Theo said. She turned around, keeping her grip on Renée. "I'm so sorry."

"Yeah, me too. Grant said something about his boys waiting downstairs…"

Theo made a dismissive gesture. "A couple of his minions."

"You heard from Vanessa?"

"Yes. They're okay. We arrested the guy who was on the way to the safehouse."

Her own eyes were welling up too. Joanna cleared her throat.

"I guess you're going to need my statement. She should go to the hospital."

"I agree. And we'll take you too."

Joanna was about to protest, but when she reached up to wipe her face, she noticed the red smear on her hand.

"So, you got my message."

"Yes, I did." Theo waited until a couple of paramedics had arrived and started to tend to Renée.

He laid an arm around her shoulders. "Let's get you out of here."

<hr/>

Cleaned and patched up, Joanna sat on the edge of the examination table when the curtain was drawn back, and a moment later, Rue held her tightly.

"I am so sorry," she said. Joanna's stomach lurched, but then she saw Vanessa waving from a distance. Mary was with her.

"You're all right. That's all I need to know." She sensed Rue's hesitation, but Joanna wasn't sure how to ease her mind. She should react somehow. Cry? She couldn't bring herself to do that, not yet. Regrets? For sure, because Lawrence had managed to manipulate her one last time. If her involvement did anything to save Renée Madison, she didn't regret it. Unlike what she'd been accused of, Joanna didn't discriminate because of political beliefs.

Rue sat back, taking both of her hands.

"I know this has been a lot," she said. "But we need to talk."

"You don't have to worry. This will be cleared up easily. I sent a message to Theo from the car, but Lawrence...I didn't know all of it. I had no idea he saw all of this as a challenge. He knew they had her."

"He knew a lot more than that," Rue said somberly. "But Mary should be the one to tell you."

# Chapter Sixteen

When she was younger, Joanna had often dreamed about what it would be like to find her mother. In later years, suspicion and cynicism, toward her family and the world in general, had been seeping in.

The reality was like nothing she'd ever imagined. Mary had made mistakes. Lawrence had played people to what he perceived as his advantage to the very end.

"There's a lot to think about now," Mary reminded her gently as they sat in a quiet corner of the hotel bar. Joanna would have liked to retreat to the room with Rue, but they still needed to eat, and apparently, she still needed to have this conversation.

Might as well get it over with.

Pain medication and a couple of Martinis had mellowed her disbelief, anger, and grief for the moment. Rue had not argued, knowing what kind of revelations Mary had for her.

"I don't know," Joanna said. "We'll go home tomorrow as planned. I might have to come back to testify against Grant, which I'll gladly do, but that's it. Dad wrote me out of the will a long time ago, so I don't expect any surprises there."

Not that she'd ever been after his money. All Joanna had wanted was some basic human respect. She'd never gotten it from Lawrence Mitchell, and the only time he'd been fairly polite was when he needed something from her.

The story ended there.

She felt her throat tighten, but that might be more from the physical violence she'd endured rather than emotion.

"Lawrence wasn't always like that. Money and power corrupted him."

"He kept you in a prison without walls. With his money, Grant, and everyone he paid off or did shady deals with..." Joanna shook her head. "No. I can't ever make excuses for men like this, not even my own father."

Mary didn't try to argue.

"You're free now. What are you going to do?"

"I'm not sure. Jeff, Terry, Lawrence, they're all gone." Mary's eyes glistened with tears. "I guess I have to sit down with my band, see where we go from here. I actually have to start making decisions for myself."

Or maybe it was emotion seeping into her tone, into her mind, for all the time lost, for something that could never be returned.

"Mom. You didn't deserve any of this."

"I wanted this other life. With you, and Ethan."

"I know. I think...I remember him a little. I am so sorry."

"Thank you." Mary took a tissue out of her purse and washed her face.

They couldn't turn back time, but they could acknowledge what was real. Joanna could live with that.

"I would have come with you if I'd had a choice. But there's something I've been meaning to ask you for a while."

"Ask away," Mary said. "I can't think of any more secrets I need to keep."

"It's not a secret, but...Would you like to come to our wedding?"

Mary enveloped her in a hug tight enough to remind her of every bruise she'd gotten today. Joanna didn't care.

The day they'd been dreaming about had arrived, and it came with a number of realizations.

Joanna had once intended to make a difference in the world. Had she? If she'd learned anything in the past years, it was that dreams and motivations could change. She wouldn't feel remorse over ending a killer's life, but her regrets would always be for the pain she'd caused others in the wake of her ambitions, or the lives that didn't change as profoundly as she'd hoped.

She had never even dreamed about a wedding, and a white dress, but Mary had arrived early to go shopping with her.

With Rue by her side, her wife—and more friends to celebrate with than she'd ever imagined—Joanna felt truly happy. She wasn't sure if it was something she'd ever had experienced or taken the time to do so.

Zach and Dr. Shepherd were present, reminding her that she, too, had unfinished business, issues to tackle. But she and Rue were home, and safe.

Mary was no longer living under Lawrence's thumb. Kira was the surprise guest.

It was likely Vanessa had something to do with it.

There was someone Joanna didn't expect. She all but jumped to her feet when Renée Madison came up behind her.

"Ms. Madison," she said. "I have many questions. How are you? And what are you doing here?"

Given the fact that they'd escaped a life-threatening situation together, she held back a sarcastic remark about how surprising it really was to see Renée on a day two women said *I do* to each other.

"I won't bother you for long," Renée said, her tone impassive, not giving Joanna any clue. "You know that Lawrence wrote you out of the will."

"Yes, I do. You came all the way to tell me this on my wedding day?"

"He left a lot of money to conservative organizations. Some that I agree with, some that are out of bounds."

"I still don't see the surprise."

"He left the lion share, and his business, to me."

Joanna could feel her jaw drop. Had he loved someone after all?

Renée shook her head. "I don't need the money, at least not that much, and I already have a job I like doing. It's because of you that I'm not dead and instead able to keep doing that job, so I figured I owed you. I'm going to take my share and run. After everything Lawrence has done, I think you and Mary should be the ones to get most out of it and decide what to do with the business."

Joanna was still speechless, so Rue, who had joined them, spoke.

"This is very generous. Do we have to worry about a catch?"

"I'm sure you're aware what it's like to be scared to death," Renée told her. "It puts a lot of things into perspective, doesn't it?" She produced a folder she laid on the table. "Have those looked over by your lawyer, and sign as soon as possible. I'll be here for a few days. God knows I deserve a vacation."

"Thank you," Joanna finally said, still dumbfounded. Renée got up and left, and Rue sat in her place.

"Wow. Are you going to be CEO?"

"No way in hell. I'll talk to Mary, and we'll figure out how to sell. My share anyway, she's free to do whatever with hers."

Vanessa came over to them, a glass of champagne in hand. "Happy Wedding Day," she said.

"Thank you. And thank you for everything you've done for us. We'll never be able to repay you."

"No need, I was happy to do it. There's something I wanted to talk to you about. Alexandra and Tamara send their best wishes." She didn't give Joanna and Rue any time to process. "I hear you got a generous gift," Vanessa continued. "I have an idea what you could do with all that money."

Rue and Joanna shared a look. They hadn't figured out yet why Vanessa had been able to intervene in Mary's story, or why she'd managed to help Joanna and Rue start their life on the island. Everything regarding her actions had been vague and mysterious, and probably they didn't want to dig too deeply for the fear it could all fall apart.

There was no reason to be afraid any longer. Vanessa obviously had ways to help women in desperate situations, with her friend who had arranged for them to leave the country, the security staff guarding Mary in the safehouse.

"Yeah, it's not like we have all that money yet. How come you know about this anyway?"

Vanessa smiled as if she thought Joanna could answer that question all by herself.

"Someday we need to have a good long talk about what you've been doing since you left IA."

"So, you'd be ready to invest in a worthy cause?" Vanessa ventured.

"If it's about freeing women from the influence of people like Lawrence, there's poetic justice in it. I'd like to hear more about it."

Perhaps, more than one dream of hers would come true, now that she and Rue were finally home.

# About the Author

B arbara Winkes writes sapphic crime drama and Christmas romance. She loves writing characters who get the job done, whether it's stopping a predator or saving cherished traditions—while still making time for love. She lives with her wife in Quebec City.

barbarawinkes.com

# Also by Barbara Winkes

**Luce Allen Mysteries**
*In Harm's Way*
*Under Pressure*

**The Crossing Lines Trilogy**
*Undercover*
*Redemption*
*Vengeance*

**The Connected Series**
*Promised to the Queen*
*Drawn to the Enemy*
*Tempted by the Protector*
*Saved by the Heiress*

**Carpenter/Harding**
*Indiscretions*
*Insinuations*
*Incisions*
*Intrusions*

BARBARA WINKES

*Initiations*
*Intentions*
*Infatuations*
*Impressions*
*Implications*
*Infractions*
*Incidents*
*Illusions*

## Kelli & Merin Romantic Suspense
*Thunder*
*Rain*

### *Lord and Burton*
*Clean Slate*

### Standalone
*The Amnesia Project*